THE
CROWN

ALSO BY KIERA CASS

The Selection
The Elite
The One
The Heir
Happily Ever After: Companion to the Selection Series

The Siren

THE CROWN

KIERA CASS

HARPER TEEN
An Imprint of HarperCollinsPublishers

HarperTeen is an imprint of HarperCollins Publishers.

The Crown
Copyright © 2016 by Kiera Cass
All rights reserved. Printed in the United States of America.
No part of this book may be used or reproduced in any manner
whatsoever without written permission except in the case of brief
quotations embodied in critical articles and reviews. For information
address HarperCollins Children's Books, a division of HarperCollins
Publishers, 195 Broadway, New York, NY 10007.
www.epicreads.com

Library of Congress Control Number: 2016930379
ISBN 978-0-06-239217-6 (trade bdg.)
ISBN 978-0-06-247928-0 (special edition)
ISBN 978-0-06-245886-5 (int.)
ISBN 978-0-06-256104-6 (special edition)

Typography by Sarah Hoy
16 17 18 19 20 CG/RRDH 10 9 8 7 6 5 4 3 2 1

First Edition

For Guyden and Zuzu,
the best little characters I ever made up.

CHAPTER 1

"I'M SORRY," I SAID, BRACING myself for the inevitable back-lash. When my Selection started, I'd pictured it ending this way—with dozens of my suitors leaving at a time, many of them unprepared for their moment in the spotlight to be over. But after the last few weeks, after learning how kind, how smart, how generous so many of them were, I found the mass elimination almost heartbreaking.

They'd been fair with me, and now I had to be very unfair to them. The live announcement would make the elimination official, and they all had to wait until then.

"I know it's abrupt, but given my mother's precarious condition, my father has asked me to take on more responsibilities, and I feel the only way to manage that is to scale down this competition."

"How is the queen?" Hale asked, swallowing hard.

I sighed. "She looks . . . she looks pretty bad."

Dad had been hesitant to let me visit her, but I had finally worn him down. I understood his reluctance the instant I saw her, asleep, the metronome of her heartbeat keeping time on the monitor. She'd just come out of surgery, where the doctors had to harvest a vein from her leg to replace the one in her chest that had been worked to death.

One of the doctors said they had lost her for a minute but managed to get her back. I sat beside her, holding her hand. Silly as it sounded, I had slouched in my chair, certain that would make her come to and correct my posture. It didn't.

"She's alive though. And my father . . . he's . . ."

Raoul placed a comforting hand on my shoulder. "It's okay, Your Highness. We all understand."

I let my eyes flit across the space, my gaze settling on each of my suitors for a breath as I committed their faces to memory.

"For the record, I was terrified of you," I confessed. There were a few chuckles around the room. "Thank you so much for taking this chance, and for being so gracious with me."

A guard entered, clearing his throat to announce his presence. "I'm sorry, my lady. It's nearly time for the broadcast. The crew wanted to check, um"—he made a fumbling gesture with his hand—"hair and stuff."

I nodded. "Thank you. I'll be ready in a moment."

After he left, I turned my attention back to the boys. "I hope you'll forgive me for this group good-bye. I wish you all the best of luck in the future."

There was a chorus of murmured good-byes as I left.

Once I was outside the doors of the Men's Parlor, I took a deep breath and prepared myself for what was coming. *You are Eadlyn Schreave and no one—literally, no one—is as powerful as you.*

The palace was eerily quiet without Mom and her ladies scuttling around and Ahren's laughter filling the halls. Nothing makes you quite so aware of a person's presence as the loss of it.

I held myself tall as I made my way down to the studio.

"Your Highness," several people greeted me as I came through the doorway, curtsying and moving out of my way, all the while avoiding looking directly in my eyes. I couldn't tell if it was out of sympathy or if they already knew.

"Oh," I said, glancing in the mirror. "I am a bit shiny. Could you—?"

"Of course, Your Highness." A girl expertly dabbed at my skin, covering me in powder.

I straightened the high lace collar of my gown. When I'd gotten dressed this morning, black seemed appropriate, considering the overall mood in the palace, but I was second-guessing myself.

"I look too serious," I worried aloud. "Not respectable serious, but worried serious. This is all wrong."

"You look beautiful, my lady." The makeup girl swept a fresh splash of color across my lips. "Like your mother."

"No, I don't," I lamented. "Not a stitch of her hair or skin or eyes."

"That's not what I mean." The girl, warm and round, with

wisps of curls falling across her forehead, stood beside me and gazed at my reflection. "See there," she said, pointing to my eyes. "Not the same color, but the same determination. And your lips, they have the same hopeful smile. I know you have your grandmother's coloring, but you're your mother's daughter, through and through."

I stared at myself. I could almost see what she meant. At this most isolating moment, I felt a little less alone.

"Thank you. That means a great deal to me."

"We're all praying for her, my lady. She's a tough one."

I giggled in spite of my mood. "That she is."

"Two minutes!" the floor director called. I walked onto the carpeted set, smoothing out my gown and touching my hair. The studio was colder than usual, even under the lights, and goose bumps prickled at my skin as I took my place behind the lone podium.

Gavril, slightly dressed down but still very polished, gave me a sympathetic smile as he approached. "Are you sure you want to do this? I'm happy to deliver the news for you."

"Thank you, but I think I have to do it on my own."

"All right then. How's she holding up?"

"Okay as of an hour ago. The doctors are keeping her asleep so she can heal, but she looks so battered." I closed my eyes for a moment, calming myself. "Sorry. This has me a bit on edge. But at least I'm managing better than Dad."

He shook his head. "I can't imagine anyone taking this worse than him. His whole world has hung on her since they met."

I thought back to last night, to the wall of photos in their room, and I thumbed through all the details they'd only recently divulged about how they got together. I still couldn't see any rhyme or reason to fighting through countless obstacles for love only to have it leave you so powerless in the end.

"You were there, Gavril. You saw their Selection." I swallowed, still unsure. "Does it really work? How?"

He shrugged. "Yours is the third I've seen, and I can't tell you how it works, how a lottery can bring in a soul mate. Let me say this: Your grandfather was not exactly a man I admired, but he treated his queen as if she was the most important person to walk the planet. Where he was harsh with others, he was generous with her. She got the best of him, which is more than I can say for . . . Well, he found the right woman."

I squinted, curious about what he was omitting. I knew Grandpa had been a strict ruler, but come to think of it, that was the only way I knew him. Dad didn't talk about him much as a husband or father, and I'd always been much more interested in hearing about Grandma.

"And your dad? I don't think he had a clue what he was looking for. Honestly, I don't think your mother did either. But she was his match in every way. Everyone around them could see it long before they did."

"Really?" I asked. "They didn't know?"

He made a face. "Truthfully, it was more that she didn't know." He gave me a pointed look. "A family trait, it seems."

"Gavril, you're one of the few people I can confess this to. It's not that I don't know what I'm looking for. It's that I wasn't ready to look."

"Ah. I wondered."

"But now I'm here."

"And on your own, I'm afraid. If you choose to go through with this—and after yesterday, no one would blame you if you didn't—only you can make such an important choice."

I nodded. "I know. Which is why this is so scary."

"Ten seconds," the floor director called.

Gavril patted my shoulder. "I'm here in whatever way I can be, Your Highness."

"Thank you."

I squared my shoulders in front of the camera, trying to look calm as the light began glowing red.

"Good morning, people of Illéa. I, Princess Eadlyn Schreave, am here to address some recent events that have taken place in the royal family. I shall deliver the good news first." I tried to smile, really I did, but all I could think of was how abandoned I felt.

"My beloved brother, Prince Ahren Schreave, has married Princess Camille de Sauveterre of France. Though the timing of their wedding was a bit of a surprise, it in no way lessens our joy for the happy couple. I hope you will join me in wishing them both the happiest of marriages."

I paused. *You can do this, Eadlyn.*

"In sadder news, last night, my mother, America Schreave, queen of Illéa, suffered a very serious heart attack."

I paused. The words felt like they had created a dam in my throat, making it harder and harder to speak.

"She is in critical condition and is under constant medical supervision. Please pr—"

I brought my hand to my mouth. I was going to cry. I was going to lose it on national television, and on top of everything Ahren had said about how people felt about me, appearing weak was the last thing I wanted.

I looked down. Mom needed me. Dad needed me. Maybe, in a small way, even the country needed me. I couldn't disappoint them. Dabbing away the tears, I went on.

"Please pray for her speedy recovery, as we all adore her and still depend on her guidance."

I breathed. It was the only way to get from any moment to the next. Breathe in, breathe out.

"My mother held such great respect for the Selection, which, as you all know, led to my parents' long and happy marriage. As such, I've decided to honor what I know would be her deepest wish and continue with my own Selection.

"Due to the stress placed on our household in the last twenty-four hours, I think it wise to cut my suitors down to the Elite. My father narrowed his field to six instead of ten because of extenuating circumstances, and I have done the same. The following six gentlemen have been invited to stay on in the Selection: Sir Gunner Croft, Sir Kile Woodwork, Sir Ean Cabel, Sir Hale Garner, Sir Fox Wesley, and Sir Henri Jaakoppi."

These names were a strangely comforting thing, like I

knew how proud they were of this moment and I could feel the glow of it, even from a distance.

It was almost done. They knew Ahren was gone, that my mother might die, and that the Selection would carry on. Now came the news I was terrified to deliver. Thanks to Ahren, I understood exactly what my people thought of me. What kind of response would I receive?

"With my mother in such a delicate state, my father, King Maxon Schreave, has chosen to remain by her side." *Here goes.* "As such, he has named me regent until he feels fit to reclaim his title. I will make all decisions of state until further notice. It is with a heavy heart that I assume this role, but it gives me great joy to bring any peace to my parents.

"We will have more updates on all these matters as they become available. Thank you for your time, and good day."

The cameras stopped rolling, and I moved just off the stage, sitting in one of the chairs that were usually reserved for my family. I felt queasy and would have sat there for hours trying to regain my composure if I thought I could get away with it, but there was too much to do. The first thing on the list was to check on Mom and Dad again, then off to work. At some point today I would have to meet with the Elite as well.

As I went to exit the studio, I stopped short because my path was blocked by a row of gentlemen. The first face I saw was Hale's. His expression lit up as he held out a flower. "For you."

I looked down the line and saw they all had flowers in

their hands, some with roots still noticeably attached. All I could assume was that they had heard their names on the announcement, rushed from the Men's Parlor to the garden, and come down here.

"You idiots," I sighed. "Thank you."

I took Hale's flower and hugged him. "I know I said something every day," he whispered, "but let me know if you need me to up it to two, okay?"

I held him a little tighter. "Thanks."

Ean was next, and though we'd only ever touched during those staged photos of our date, I found myself unable to refrain from embracing him.

"I get the feeling you were coerced into this," I murmured.

"I took mine from a vase in the hallway. Don't tell the staff on me."

I patted his back, and he did the same to me.

"She'll be okay," he promised. "You all will."

Kile had pricked his finger on a thorn and held his bleeding hand awkwardly away from my clothes as we hugged, which made me laugh and was perfect.

"For smiles," Henri said as I added his flower to my messy bouquet.

"Good, good," I replied, and he laughed at me.

Even Erik had gotten me a flower. I smirked a bit as I took it.

"This is a dandelion," I told him.

He shrugged. "I know. Some see a weed; some see a flower. Perspective."

I wrapped my arms around him, and I could feel him looking at the others as I held him, seeming uncomfortable to be getting the same treatment as they had.

Gunner swallowed, not able to say much, but held me gently before I moved on.

Fox had three flowers in his hand. "I couldn't pick."

I smiled. "They're all beautiful. Thanks."

Fox's embrace was tight, like he needed the support more than the others did. I held on to him as I looked back at my Elite.

No, this whole process made no sense, but I could see how it happened, how your heart could get swept up in the endeavor. And that was my hope now: that somehow duty and love would overlap, and I'd find myself happy in the middle of it all.

CHAPTER 2

MOM'S HANDS FELT SO SOFT, almost papery in a way. The feeling made me think of how water smoothed out the edges of a stone. I smiled, thinking she must have been a very rough stone once upon a time.

"Did you ever used to get it wrong?" I asked. "Say the wrong words, do the wrong things?"

I waited for an answer, receiving nothing but the hum of equipment and the beat of the monitor.

"Well, you and Dad used to fight, so you must have been wrong sometimes."

I held her hand tighter, trying to warm it in mine.

"I made all the announcements. Now everyone knows about Ahren getting married and that you're a little . . . indisposed at the moment. I cut the boys down to six. I know that's a big cut, but Dad said it was okay and that he did that when it was his turn, so no one can get upset." I sighed. "Regardless, I have a feeling people will still find a way to get upset with me."

I blinked back tears, worried she'd sense how scared I was. The doctors believed that the shock of Ahren's departure was the catalyst for her current condition, though I couldn't help but wonder if I'd contributed to her stress daily, like drops of poison so small someone didn't realize they'd ingested something dangerous until it had overtaken them.

"Anyway, I'm off to run my first advisory board meeting as soon as Dad gets back. He says it shouldn't be too difficult. Honestly, I feel like General Leger had the toughest job of anyone today, trying to get Dad to go eat, because he fought so hard to stay here with you. The general was insistent, though, and Dad finally caved. I'm glad he's here. General Leger, I mean. It's kind of like having a backup parent."

I held her hand a little tighter and leaned in, whispering. "Please don't make me need a backup parent, though, okay? I still need you. The boys still need you. And Dad . . . he looks like he might fall apart if you leave. So when it's time to wake up, you've gotta come back, all right?"

I waited for her mouth to twitch or her fingers to move, anything to show that she could hear me. Nothing.

Just then Dad tore through the door with General Leger on his heels. I wiped at my cheeks, hoping no one would notice.

"See," General Leger said. "She's stable. The doctors would come running if anything changed."

"All the same, I prefer to be here," Dad said firmly.

"Dad, you were hardly gone ten minutes. Did you even eat?"

"I ate. Tell her, Aspen."

General Leger sighed. "We'll call it eating."

Dad shot him a look that would have been threatening to some but only made the general smile. "I'll see if I can sneak some food in so you won't have to leave."

Dad nodded. "Look out for my girl."

"Of course." General Leger winked at me, and I stood up and followed him from the room, looking back at Mom just to check.

Still asleep.

In the hallway, he held out an arm for me. "You ready, my not-quite queen?"

I took it and smiled. "No. Let's go."

As we made our way to the boardroom, I nearly asked General Leger if he would take me for another lap around the floor. The day felt so overwhelming already that I wasn't sure I could do this.

Nonsense, I told myself. *You've sat in on these meetings dozens of times. You've almost always thought the same things Dad has said. Yes, this is your first time leading it, but this was always waiting for you. And no one is going to be hard on you today, for goodness' sake; your mother just had a heart attack.*

I pulled the door open with purpose, General Leger trailing behind me. I made sure to nod at the gentlemen as I passed. Sir Andrews, Sir Coddly, Mr. Rasmus, and a handful of other men I'd known for years sat arranging their pens and paper. Lady Brice looked proud as she watched me sweep around to my father's spot, as did the general when he settled into the place beside her.

"Good morning." I took my seat at the head of the table, gazing down at the thin folder in front of me. Thank goodness the agenda looked light today.

"How is your mother?" Lady Brice asked solemnly.

I should have written this answer on a sign so I could stop repeating it. "She's asleep still. I'm not sure how serious her condition is at the moment, but Dad is staying by her side, and we'll be sure to update everyone if there's any change."

Lady Brice smiled sadly. "I'm sure she'll be fine. She always was a tough one."

I tried to hide my surprise, but I didn't realize Lady Brice knew my mother that well. In truth, I didn't know that much about Lady Brice myself, but her tone was so sincere, I was happy to have her beside me at the moment.

I nodded. "Let's get through this so I can tell her my first day on the job was at least slightly productive."

There were gentle chuckles around the room at that, but my smile quickly faded as I read the first page presented to me.

"I hope this is a joke," I said dryly.

"No, Your Highness."

I turned my eyes to Sir Coddly.

"We feel this was a deliberate move to debilitate Illéa, and seeing as neither the king nor queen gave their consent,

France has essentially stolen your brother. This marriage is treasonous, so we have no choice but to go to war."

"Sir, I assure you, this was not treasonous. Camille is a sensible girl." I rolled my eyes, hating to admit it. "It's Ahren who's the romantic one, and I feel certain he urged her into this, not the other way around."

I balled up the declaration of war, unwilling to consider it for another moment.

"My lady, you cannot do that," Sir Andrew insisted. "The relations between Illéa and France have been tense for years."

"That is more on a personal level than a political one," Lady Brice offered.

Sir Coddly waved his hand in the air. "Which makes this all much worse. Queen Daphne is brandishing more emotional suffering on the royal family under the assumption that we will not respond. This time we must. Tell her, general!"

Lady Brice shook her head in frustration as General Leger spoke. "All I will say, Your Highness, is that we can have troops in the sky and on the ground within twenty-four hours if you command it. Though I certainly wouldn't *advise* you to make that command."

Andrews huffed. "Leger, tell her the dangers she's facing."

He shrugged. "I see no danger here. Her brother got married."

"If anything," I questioned, "shouldn't a wedding bring our two countries closer? Isn't that why princesses were married off for years?"

"But those were planned," Coddly stated in a tone that implied I was a little too naive for the conversation at hand.

"As was this," I countered. "We all knew Ahren and Camille would wed one day. It simply happened sooner than expected."

"She doesn't get it," he muttered to Andrews.

Sir Andrews shook his head at me. "Your Highness, this is treason."

"Sir, this is love."

Coddly slammed a fist on the table. "No one will take you seriously if you do not act decisively."

There was a beat of silence after his voice stopped echoing around the room, and the entire table sat motionless.

"Fine," I responded calmly. "You're fired."

Coddly laughed, looking at the other gentlemen at the table. "You can't fire me, Your Highness."

I tilted my head, staring at him. "I assure you, I can. There's no one here who outranks me at the moment, and you are easily replaceable."

Though she tried to be discreet, I saw Lady Brice purse her lips together, clearly determined not to laugh. Yes, I definitely had an ally in her.

"You need to fight!" he insisted.

"No," I answered firmly. "A war would add unnecessary strain to an already stressful moment and would cause an upheaval between us and the country we are now bound to by marriage. We will not fight."

Coddly lowered his chin and squinted. "Don't you think you're being too emotional about this?"

I stood, my chair screeching behind me as I moved. "I'm going to assume that you aren't implying by that statement that I'm actually being too *female* about this. Because, yes, I am emotional."

I strode around the opposite side of the table, my eyes trained on Coddly. "My mother is in a bed with tubes down her throat, my twin is now on a different continent, and my father is holding himself together by a thread."

Stopping across from him, I continued. "I have two younger brothers to keep calm in the wake of all this, a country to run, and six boys downstairs waiting for me to offer one of them my hand." Coddly swallowed, and I felt only the tiniest bit of guilt for the satisfaction it brought me. "So, yes, I am emotional right now. Anyone in my position with a soul would be. And you, sir, are an idiot. How dare you try to force my hand on something so monumental on the grounds of something so small? For all intents and purposes, I am queen, and you will not coerce me into anything."

I walked back to the head of the table. "Officer Leger?"

"Yes, Your Highness?"

"Is there anything on this agenda that can't wait until tomorrow?"

"No, Your Highness."

"Good. You're all dismissed. And I suggest you all remember who's in charge here before we meet again."

As soon as I finished speaking, everyone other than Lady Brice and General Leger rose and bowed—rather deeply, I noted.

"You were wonderful, Your Highness," Lady Brice insisted once the three of us were alone.

"I was? Look at my hand." I held it up.

"You're trembling."

I pulled my fingers into a fist, determined to stop shaking. "Everything I said was true, right? They can't force me to sign a declaration of war, can they?"

"No," General Leger assured me. "As you know, there have always been a few members of the board who have thought we should colonize in Europe. I think they saw this as an opportunity to take advantage of your limited experience, but you did everything right."

"Dad wouldn't want to go to war. The banner of his reign has been peace."

"Exactly." General Leger smiled. "He'd be proud of how you stood your ground. In fact, I think I might just go tell him."

"Should I go, too?" I asked, suddenly desperate to hear the little monitor announcing that Mom's heart was still there, still trying.

"You have a country to run. I'll bring you an update as soon as I can."

"Thank you," I called as he exited the room.

Lady Brice crossed her arms on the table. "Feeling better?"

I shook my head. "I knew this role would be a lot of work.

I've done my share of it and watched my dad do ten times what I did. But I was supposed to have more time to get ready. To start the job now, because my mom might die, is too much. And within five minutes of being responsible, I have to make a decision about war? I'm not prepared for this."

"Okay, first things first. You don't have to be perfect yet. This is temporary. Your mom will get better, your dad will come back to work, and you will go back to learning with this great experience under your belt. Think of this time as an opportunity."

I let out a long breath. Temporary. Opportunity. Okay.

"Besides, it's not all completely up to you. This is what your advisers are for. Granted, they weren't much help today, but we're here so you aren't navigating without a map."

I bit my lip, thinking. "Okay. So, what do I do now?"

"First, follow through and fire Coddly. It will show the others you mean what you say. I do feel somewhat bad for him, but I think your father only kept him around to play devil's advocate and help him see all sides of an issue. Trust me, he won't be sorely missed," she confessed dryly. "Second, consider this time a period of hands-on training for your reign. Start surrounding yourself with people you know you can trust."

I sighed. "I feel like they've all just left me."

She shook her head. "Look closer. You probably have friends in places you never expected."

Again, I found myself seeing her in a new light. She'd stayed in her role longer than anyone; she knew what Dad would decide in most situations; and she was, at the very least, another woman in the room.

Lady Brice stared into my eyes, forcing me to focus. "Who do you know will always be honest with you? Who will be by your side, not because you're royal, but because you're you?"

I smiled, absolutely positive of where I was going once I left this room.

CHAPTER 3

"ME?"

"You."

"Are you sure?"

I grabbed Neena by the shoulders. "You always tell me the truth, even if I'm not excited to hear it. You've put up with the worst of me, and you're too clever to spend your days folding my laundry."

She beamed, blinking to quell her tears. "A lady-in-waiting . . . what does that even mean?"

"Well, it's a mix of being a companion, which you already are, and then helping with the less glamorous side of my job, like scheduling appointments and making sure I remember to eat."

"I think I can handle that," she said, smiling.

"Oh, oh, oh, and"—I held up my hands, preparing her for probably the most exciting part of the job—"it means you don't have to wear that uniform anymore. So go change."

Neena chuckled. "I don't know that I have anything appropriate. But I'll make sure to get something together for tomorrow."

"Nonsense. Just go through my closet."

She gaped at me. "I can't."

"Umm, you can and you must." I pointed to the wide doors. "Get dressed, meet me in the office, and we'll make it through whatever comes one day at a time."

She nodded, and, as if we'd done it a thousand times, she threw her arms around me.

"Thank you."

"Thank *you*," I insisted.

"I won't let you down."

I pulled back, watching her. "I know. By the way, your first job is to pick a new maid for me."

"Not a problem."

"Excellent. I'll see you soon."

I swept from the room, feeling better knowing I had people on my side. General Leger would be my line to Mom and Dad, Lady Brice would be my chief adviser, and Neena would help me shoulder the workload.

It had been less than a day, and I already understood why Mom thought I'd need a partner. And I still intended to find one. I just needed a little time to figure out how.

★ ★ ★

That afternoon I paced worriedly as I waited for Kile outside the Men's Parlor. Of all my relationships with the Selected, ours felt the most complicated and yet the easiest place to start.

"Hey," he said, coming to embrace me. I couldn't help smiling thinking about how if he'd tried that a month ago, I'd have called the guards on him. "How are you doing?"

I paused. "It's funny—you're the only one who's asked." We stepped apart. "I'm okay, I think. At least I am as long as I'm busy. The second things slow down, I'm a ball of nerves. Dad's a wreck. And it's killing me that Ahren hasn't come back. I thought he would for Mom, but he hasn't even called. Shouldn't he at least have done that?"

I swallowed, knowing I was getting too worked up.

Kile took my hand. "Okay, let's think about this. He flew to France and got married in one day. There has to be a ton of official paperwork and other stuff to sort through. And there's a chance he hasn't even heard what happened."

I nodded. "You're right. And I know he cares. He left me a letter, and it was too honest for me to question that."

"See, there you go. And last night your dad looked like he was two seconds away from needing to be checked into the hospital wing himself. Being with your mom and monitoring her probably gives him a feeling of control when there's absolutely none. She's made it through the worst, and she's always been a fighter. Remember when that one ambassador came?"

I smirked. "You mean the one from the Paraguay-Argentina Union?"

"Yes!" he exclaimed. "I can still picture it perfectly. He was so rude to everyone, falling down drunk by noon two days in a row, and your mom finally grabbed him by the ear and dragged him out the front door."

I shook my head. "I do. I also remember the endless phone calls afterward trying to smooth things over with their president."

Kile brushed that detail away. "Forget that. Just remember, your mother doesn't let things happen to her. When something tries to ruin her life, she drags it into the street."

I smiled. "True."

We stood there, quiet for a moment, and it was pleasant and still. I'd never been so grateful. "I'm busy the rest of today, but maybe we could spend some time together tomorrow night?"

He nodded. "Of course."

"There's a lot to talk about."

His eyebrows knit together. "Like what?"

We both turned at the same time, noting the figure in our periphery.

"Excuse me, Your Highness," the guard said with a bow, "but you have a visitor."

"A visitor?"

He nodded, giving me no information as to who it might be.

I sighed. "Fine. I'll get in touch later, okay?"

Kile gave my hand a quick squeeze. "Sure. Let me know if you need anything."

I smiled as I left him, knowing that he meant that. In the back of my mind, I felt certain all the young men in that room would rush to my side if I needed them to, and that was a small silver lining on an otherwise dreary day.

I rounded the stairs, trying to guess at who was here. If it had been family, they'd have been brought to a room; and if it was a governor or some other official visitor, they'd have sent up a card. Who was so important that they couldn't even be announced?

As I descended to the first floor, the answer to my question stood there, his bright smile making my breath catch.

Marid Illéa hadn't set foot in the palace in years. The last time I'd laid eyes on him, he was a gangly preteen who hadn't quite mastered conventional conversation. But his round cheeks had turned into a jaw line sharp enough to cut, and his stringy limbs had filled out, hitting the seams of his suit with perfect precision. He held my gaze as I approached, and even though his hands were full with an overflowing basket, he bowed and smiled as if he was completely unencumbered.

"Your Highness," he said. "I'm sorry to come unannounced, but as soon as we heard about your mother, we felt we had to do something. So . . ."

He held out the basket toward me. It was full of gifts. Flowers, thin books, jars of soup with ribbons around the lids, and even a few bakery items that looked so good it was hard not to take one for myself.

"Marid," I said, a greeting, a question, and an admonition all at once. "This is above and beyond, all things considered."

He shrugged. "Disagreements don't mean a loss of compassion. Our queen is sick, and this was the least we could do."

I smiled, moved by his sudden appearance. I motioned to a guard.

"Take this to the hospital wing, please."

He took the gift basket, and I turned my focus back to Marid.

"Your parents didn't want to come?"

He shoved his hands into his pockets and grimaced. "They were afraid the visit would seem more political than personal."

I nodded. "Understandable. But please tell them not to worry about that in the future. They're still welcome here."

Marid sighed. "They didn't think so, not after their . . . exit."

I pressed my lips together, remembering it all so clearly.

August Illéa and my father had worked together closely after my grandparents died, trying to dissolve the castes as quickly as they could. When August complained that change wasn't happening fast enough, Dad pulled rank and told him to respect his plan. When Dad couldn't quite erase the stigma of being in the lower castes, August said he needed to get his "spoiled ass" out of the palace and into the streets. Dad had always been a patient man, and, from what I remembered of August, he was always on edge. In the end there was a big fight, and August and Georgia packed their things, including their bashful son, and left in a hurricane of hurt and anger.

I'd heard Marid's voice once or twice on the radio since then, giving political commentary or business advice, but it was strange now, having that voice sync up to the movements of his lips and seeing him smile so easily when I mostly remembered him slouched over himself when he was younger.

"Honestly, I don't understand why our fathers haven't spoken recently. You've certainly seen the issues with the post-caste discrimination we've been trying to quell. I thought one of them might break and seek out the other. It's past being a point of pride anymore."

Marid extended an arm. "Perhaps we could walk and talk?"

I linked my arm through his, and we began moving down the hall.

"How is it going so far?"

I shrugged. "As best it can under the circumstances."

"I'd like to tell you to look on the bright side, but it might be hard to find one."

"So far, all I can think of is that I'm helping my parents."

"True. And who knows? You might be able to make some

serious changes while you're in office. Like all the post-caste issues. Our parents couldn't get it right, but maybe you could."

That thought comforted me less than he intended. I didn't hope to be in control long enough to make any changes at all.

"I'm not quite sure I'm capable of that."

"Well, Your Highness—"

"Please, Marid. It's Eadlyn. You've known me since before I was born."

He smirked. "Very true. Still, you are regent right now, and it feels wrong not to address you properly."

"And what should I call you?"

"Nothing but a loyal subject. I'd like to offer any help I can in this tense time. And I know the dissolution of the castes wasn't as clean as you all hoped, not even in the beginning. I've spent years lending my ear to the public. I think I've heard them very clearly, and if my commentary would be useful, please let me know."

I raised my eyebrows as I considered his words. I knew a lot more about the lives of commoners these days thanks to the Selected, but an expert on public opinion might be a perfect tool to have in my arsenal. And even if I didn't have great ambitions for my short time on the throne, something like this might show my people I cared, and that was critical. Especially considering what Ahren had said in his letter.

It hit me like a punch every time I remembered his words, but I knew he wouldn't have told me that the people despised me if he hadn't thought it would serve some good. Even though he left, I trusted that.

"Thank you, Marid. If I could do anything to ease the stress that this situation has brought to my father, it would be a huge blessing. When he's ready to come back to work, I'd like the country to be the calmest he's seen it in years. I'll be in touch."

He pulled a card out of his pocket and handed it to me. "That's my personal number. Call anytime."

I smiled. "Will your parents be upset that you're helping me? Isn't this fraternizing with the enemy?"

"No, no," he said, his tone light. "Our parents had the same goal. They simply had different methods of reaching it. And now, with your mother unwell, you shouldn't have to worry so much about things that are fixable, and the country's morale certainly is. Now more than ever, I think our parents will approve of us working together."

"Let's hope," I said. "Far too many things have been breaking lately. Some mending would do me good."

CHAPTER 4

I SLIPPED INTO THE BATH, noting there was no lavender, no bubbles, no anything to sweeten the water. Eloise was quiet and fast, but she was no Neena. I sighed. It didn't matter, I supposed, since this was little more than a small space where at last I could stop pretending I knew what I was doing. I curled my knees to my chest, finally free to weep.

What was I going to do? Ahren wasn't here to guide me anymore, and I worried I'd make mistake after mistake without him. And why hadn't he called yet? Why wasn't he on the first flight home?

What would I do if they took the tubes out of Mom's throat and she couldn't breathe on her own? I suddenly realized that even though I'd never thought of marriage and children in a specific and personal way, I'd always envisioned her dancing at my wedding and cooing over my firstborn.

What if she wasn't there to do that?

How was I supposed to step into Dad's shoes? Today had worn me down to the bone. I couldn't imagine doing this all day every day for the next few weeks, let alone the years I'd have to do it when I truly inherited the throne.

And how was I going to choose a husband? Who was the best choice? Who would the public approve of the most? Was that even a fair question to ask? Or the right one?

I wiped my eyes with the heel of my hand like a child and wished I could go back to being blissfully unaware of how much bad could pile up in a single day.

I had power and no idea how to use it. I was a ruler who didn't know how to lead. I was a twin who was on her own. I was a daughter with missing parents. I had a half dozen suitors and wasn't sure how to be in love.

The tension constricting around my heart would be enough to overwhelm anyone. I rubbed at the ache in my chest, wondering if that was how it all started for Mom. I sat up, sloshing the water, pushing the thought from my head.

You're fine. She's fine. You just have to keep going.

I got dressed and was almost ready to turn in for the night when I heard a timid knock at the door.

"Eady?" someone called.

"Osten?" He poked his head in, with Kaden right behind him, and I rushed over to them. "Are you two all right?"

"We're okay," Kaden assured me. "And we're not scared or anything."

"Not at all," Osten added.

"But we haven't heard any news about Mom, and we thought maybe you would know something."

I smacked myself in the head. "I'm sorry. I should have told you what was going on." I cursed myself, thinking of how I'd just spent twenty minutes in a bath instead of taking the time to find my brothers.

"She's recovering." I tried to choose my words carefully. "She's being kept asleep so she can heal. You know Mom. If she was awake, she'd want to chase after us to make sure we were doing everything we were supposed to. This way she'll get enough rest so that she'll be healthy when she wakes up."

"Oh." Osten's shoulders lifted, and I could see that, as much as all this was getting to me, it was even harder on them.

"What about Ahren?" Kaden picked at a hangnail, a thing I'd never seen him do.

"No word yet, but I'm sure it's just because he's getting settled in. After all, he's a married man."

Kaden's expression showed he wasn't satisfied with that answer. "Do you think he'll come back?"

I took a deep breath. "Let's not worry about that tonight. I'm sure he'll call soon, and he'll be able to tell us everything. For now, all you two need to know is, your brother is happy, your mom is going to be okay, and I have everything under control. All right?"

They smiled. "All right."

Osten's expression went from perfectly fine to completely

distraught in seconds, and his lip began to tremble. "It's my fault, isn't it?"

"What's your fault?" I got on one knee in front of him.

"Mom. It's my fault. She always told me to calm down a little more, and then she'd run her hand through her hair like she was worn out. It's my fault. I made her too tired."

"At least you didn't bother her over school so much," Kaden said quietly. "I was always bugging her for books and better tutors, and making her answer questions when she had other stuff to do. I took up all her time."

So we were all blaming ourselves. Perfect.

"Osten, don't think that. Ever," I insisted, pulling him in for a hug. "Mom is a queen. If anything, you were the least stressful part of her life. Yes, it's hard to be a mother, but she always had us to run to if she needed a laugh. And who's easily the funniest of the four of us?"

"Me." His voice was weak, but he did smile a little as he wiped his nose.

"Exactly. And Kaden, do you think Mom would rather you ask her a dozen questions or have you wander through life with the wrong answers?"

He fidgeted with his fingers some more as he thought it over. "She'd want me to come to her."

"So there you go. Let's be honest—we're a pretty intense bunch, yeah?" Osten laughed, and Kaden's expression brightened. "But whatever we put her through, it was welcome. She'd rather have forced me to learn my penmanship than never have had a daughter. She'd rather have been your living encyclopedia than not connect with us. She'd rather have begged you to sit still than have had only three children. None of this is because of us," I promised.

I waited for them to turn and run, to get past showing this tiny chink in their armor. But they didn't budge. I sighed to myself, knowing what they were hoping for and realizing I was prepared to lose some much-needed sleep on their behalf.

"Do you want to stay here tonight?"

Osten bolted over to my bed. "Yeah!"

I shook my head. What was I going to do with these boys? I crawled into bed, and Kaden pressed himself against my back as Osten rested his head on the pillow across from me. I realized that the bathroom light was still on, but I let it go. We needed a little light at the moment.

"It's not the same without Ahren," Kaden said quietly.

Osten pulled his arms in close, bundling himself up. "Yeah. It doesn't feel right."

"I know. But don't worry. We'll find a new normal. You'll see." Somehow, for them, I would make that happen.

CHAPTER 5

"GOOD MORNING, YOUR HIGHNESS."

"Good morning," I replied to the butler. "Strong coffee, please, and whatever the chef has prepared for the Elite is fine."

"Of course."

He returned with blueberry pancakes and sausage links, and a hard-boiled egg sliced in half. I picked at my meal while I skimmed the papers. There was news of bad weather in one area and some speculation over who I might marry somewhere else, but in general, it looked like the entire nation had lost the will to do much more than worry about Mom. I was grateful. I had been positive the country would revolt when I was named regent. Part of me was still worried that if I gave the slightest indication that I might fail, their hatred would slam into me without mercy.

"Good day today!" someone called. Not *someone*. I would have recognized Henri's greeting even in the grave.

I lifted my head to smile and wave at him and Erik. I kind of loved that Henri was impervious to the sadness hanging over the palace. And Erik seemed to be the hand that guided his charge back down to Earth, calm and kind, regardless of what happened around him.

Osten and Kaden walked in with Kile, their heads together as they moved. Kile was trying to make them smile—I could read it in his body language—and, for their part, they gave him small, tight-lipped grins. Ean entered with Hale and Fox, and I was pleasantly surprised to see him finally interacting with some of the others. Gunner trailed behind them as if forgotten. I'd kept him in the Elite because I couldn't shake how his poem had made me laugh. But beyond that, I hardly knew him. I was going to have to try harder with him, with all of them.

My brothers sat down together at their normal places, more subdued than usual. Seeing our family table so empty sent a pang of sadness through my whole body. That type of sorrow, the quiet, lonely kind, can take over so quickly that a person could miss it. I could see it trying to creep into my brothers now, in the way they held their heads a little lower, probably not even aware they were doing it.

"Osten?" He peeked over at me, and I could feel the Elite's eyes on us. "Do you remember the time Mom made us pancakes?"

Kaden started laughing, turning to the others to tell the

story. "Mom used to cook a lot growing up, and every once in a while she'd make food for us, just for fun. The last time she tried was maybe four years ago."

I smirked. "She knew she was out of practice, but she wanted to make us blueberry pancakes. The thing was, she wanted to arrange the berries in them so they made stars and flowers and faces. But she left the batter on the griddle so long to put the berries in that when she flipped the pancakes, they were all burned."

Osten laughed. "I do remember! I remember the crunchy pancakes!"

I heard chuckles from the Elite.

"You were so bad, though, you didn't even try one!" Kaden accused.

I nodded shamefully. "It was self-preservation."

"They were pretty good, actually. Crispy, but good." Osten took a bite of one of the pancakes in front of him. "They make these ones seem weak."

I heard one loud chuckle and saw that Fox was shaking his head. "My dad's an awful cook, too," he said, projecting his voice. "We grill a lot, and he's always saying it's 'charred.'" Fox lifted his fingers to quote the word.

"What he actually means is burned, yeah?" Gunner asked.

"Yep."

"My father," Erik said timidly. I was surprised he wanted to join in the conversation, and I found myself leaning my head on my elbow, drawn in. "He and my mother have this one dish they make for each other, and it requires frying.

The last time he made it, he left the room while it was cooking, and the smoke was so bad, they had to move in with me for two days while they aired the house out."

"Do you have a spare room?" Kile asked.

Erik shook his head. "No. So my living room became my bedroom, which was a treat when my mom woke up at six and decided to start cleaning."

Gunner laughed in agreement. "Why do parents always do that? And always on the one day you can sleep in?"

I squinted. "Can't you just ask them not to?"

Fox laughed wildly. "Maybe you can, Your Highness."

I was very aware that I was being teased, but I knew it was all in good fun.

Hale spoke up. "Speaking of which, is anyone else worried about being incredibly spoiled if you lose and have to go home after living like this?" He gestured to the table and room.

"Not me," Kile answered flatly, and the boys erupted.

The room dissolved into stories and comments, the tail end of every sentence sparking a new memory from someone else. The conversation grew so loud, the laughter so boisterous, that no one noticed the lone maid walking down the center of the floor. She curtsied and bent her face close to mine.

"Your mother is awake."

A flurry of emotions washed over me, a dozen feelings all practically unidentifiable except for the common sensation of joy.

"Thank you!" I rushed from the room, too afraid to wait for Kaden and Osten.

My feet flew down the halls, and I burst into the hospital wing, only pausing to brace myself once I reached her door. As I slowly opened it, I was aware of the heart monitor, still recording every beat, and how the pace ticked up a notch when our eyes met.

"Mom?" I whispered.

Dad looked over his shoulder, smiling though his eyes were red and brimming with tears.

"Eadlyn," Mom whispered, holding out her hand.

I went to her, the tears in my eyes blurring my vision so much I could hardly make her out.

"Hey, Mom. How are you?" I wrapped my fingers around hers, trying not to grip too tightly.

"It hurts a little." Which meant it must hurt a lot.

"Well, you just take your time feeling better, okay? No rush."

"How are you?"

I stood up taller, hoping to convince her. "I've got everything under control, and Kaden and Osten are doing great—I'm sure they're right behind me. And I have a date tonight."

"Good job, Eady." Dad grinned and turned his head back to Mom. "See, darling? I'm not even needed out there. I can stay here with you."

"Ahren?" Mom asked, taking a deep breath afterward.

I was crestfallen. As I opened my mouth to tell her we

hadn't heard from him, Dad spoke up. "He called this morning."

I stood there, stunned. "Oh?"

"He's hoping to come home soon, but he said there were some complications, though he was a little too flustered to explain what they were. He told me to tell you he loves you." I'd hoped those words were for me, but Dad was looking directly at Mom when he spoke.

"I want my son," Mom said, her voice cracking.

"I know, darling. Soon." Dad rubbed Mom's hand.

"Mama?" Osten came into the room, his face showing that he was barely containing his excitement. Kaden was sniffling, holding himself upright as if he thought himself above crying.

"Hi there." Mom managed to pull up a big smile for them, and when Osten bent down and hugged her, she made a pained face but didn't let out a sound.

"We've been very good," he promised.

Mom smiled. "Well, stop that immediately."

We laughed.

"Hi, Mom." Kaden kissed her cheek, looking afraid to touch her just yet.

She raised her hand to cup his face. She seemed to grow stronger each second simply from seeing us. I wondered what she'd have done if Ahren was here. Jump out of the bed?

"I wanted you to know that I'm okay." Her chest rose and fell aggressively, but her smile didn't falter. "I think I can go back upstairs tomorrow."

Dad nodded quickly. "Yes, if we get through today without incident, your mother can recuperate in her room."

"That's really good." Kaden's voice lifted at this news. "So you're halfway back to normal."

I didn't want to kill the hope in his eyes, or Osten's. Kaden was typically so clever, seeing around every pretense, but there was no mistaking how hard he was willing this to be true.

"Exactly," Mom said.

"Okay, everyone," Dad said. "Now that you've seen Mom, I want you to get back to your studies. We still have a country to run."

"Eadlyn gave us the day off," Osten protested.

I smiled guiltily. When we'd gotten out of bed this morning, that was my only order. I needed them to play.

Mom laughed, a weak but beautiful sound. "Such a generous queen."

"Not queen yet," I protested, thankful that the true queen still lived and spoke and smiled.

"All the same," Dad said, "your mother needs rest. I'll make sure you see her again before bedtime."

That mollified the boys, and they left, waving to Mom.

I kissed her head. "I love you."

"My girl." Her weak fingers touched my hair. "I love you."

Those words were the first bookend of my day, and I could get through the rest of it knowing Kile Woodwork would be the other.

As I left the hospital wing, I came across another Wood-work.

"Miss Marlee?" I asked.

She looked up from the bench she was sitting on, wringing a handkerchief in her hands, her face blotchy from crying.

"Are you okay?"

She smiled. "More than okay. I was so afraid she might not come back, and . . . I honestly don't know what I'd do without her. Being here, with your mom, has been my whole life."

I sat down, hugging my mother's dearest friend, and she held on to me as if I was her own daughter. Part of me felt sad, because I knew she wasn't being dramatic when she said that. One look at her scarred palms told the long story of how she'd gone from worthy competitor to wicked traitor to faithful lady. When they talked about the past, some details were glossed over, and I never pushed it because it wasn't my place. But I worried that sometimes Miss Marlee felt like my parents' pardon was still contingent on her and her husband paying it back in devotion.

"They said that you and your brothers were visiting, and I want to see her, but I didn't want to cut off your time."

"Did you see the boys leave? We're all done now. You should hurry in before she falls back asleep. I know she'd want to see you."

She wiped her cheeks again. "How do I look?"

I laughed. "Positively wretched." I squeezed her. "Go on in there. And can you try to check on them for me from time to time? I know I won't be able to come down here as often as I'd like."

"Don't you worry. I'll send updates as often as I can."

"Thank you, Miss Marlee."

After one last hug, she made her way into the hospital wing. I sighed, trying to let myself enjoy this brief moment of calm. At least for now, everything was on its way to being better.

CHAPTER 6

KILE HELD HIS HAND AGAINST the small of my back, walking me through the garden. The moon was low and full, casting shadows even in the night.

"You were spectacular this morning," he said, shaking his head. "We've all been worried about your mom, and it's so strange not having Ahren around. And Kaden? I've never seen him look so . . . bewildered."

"It's awful. He's the stable one."

"Don't worry too much. It makes sense that he'd be a little shaken right now."

I inched even closer to Kile. "I know. It's just hard to see it happen to someone who never gets shaken."

"Which is why breakfast was so great. I thought we were going to suffer through a painful meal together, unable to talk about what was happening, or even talk at all. Then you just opened it up. It was remarkable. Don't forget you have that skill." He shook his finger at me.

"What skill? Distraction?" I laughed.

"No." He wrestled with the words. "More like the means to alleviate. I mean, you've done it before. At parties or on *Reports*. You change momentum. Not everyone can do that."

We walked to the edge of the garden, where the land opened up to a wide, flat space before the forest started.

"Thanks. That means a lot. I've been worried."

"Nothing wrong with that."

"It's bigger than Mom though." I stopped and put my hands on my hips, wondering how much I should tell him. "Ahren left me a letter. Did you know that the people are displeased with the monarchy? Specifically, me? And now I'm basically in charge, and honestly, I'm not sure if they'll stand for it. I already had food thrown at me once. I've read so many awful articles about myself. . . . What if they come after me?"

"What if they do?" he joked. "It's not like there aren't other options. We could become a dictatorship—that'd put people in line. There's a federal republic, a constitutional monarchy . . . oh, maybe a theocracy! We could give every-thing over to the church."

"Kile, I'm serious! What if they depose me?"

He cradled my face in his hands. "Eadlyn, that's not going to happen."

"But it has before! That's how my grandparents died. People came into their home and killed them. And everyone worshipped my grandmother!" I could feel the tears rising. Ugh, I'd been such a weepy mess the last couple of days! I wiped them away, fumbling over his fingers in the process.

"Listen to me. That was a pocket of radicals. They're gone now, and the people out there are too busy trying to live their lives to spend time messing with yours."

"I can't bank on that," I whispered. "There were things I was always sure of, and almost all of that has fallen apart in the last few weeks."

"Do you . . ." He paused as he gazed into my eyes. "Do you need to not think right now?"

I swallowed, processing the offer. Here with just the two of us in the dark, quiet evening, it felt so similar to the night of our first kiss. Only this time there'd be no one watching, no one to print it in a newspaper. Our parents were nowhere in sight, and the guards weren't trailing our steps. For me it meant that, for just one moment, there was nothing to keep me from having what I wanted.

"I'd do anything you asked me to, Eadlyn," he whispered.

I shook my head. "But I can't ask."

He squinted. "Why not? Did I do something wrong?"

"No, you idiot," I said, pulling away. "Apparently . . ." I huffed. "It seems you did something right. I can't just kiss you like it's nothing, because it turns out that you're not nothing."

I stared at the ground, growing increasingly irritated.

"This is all your fault, by the way!" I accused, glaring at

him as I paced. "I was fine not liking you. I was fine not liking anyone." I covered my face. "And now I'm in the middle of this thing and so lost I can hardly think straight. But I know that you matter, and I don't know what to do about it." When I gathered enough courage to look up at him again, he was smirking. "For goodness' sake, don't look so smug."

"Sorry," he said, still smiling.

"Do you know how scary it is for me to say all that?"

He bridged the gap between us. "Probably as scary as it is for me to hear it."

"I'm serious, Kile."

"So am I! First of all, it's strange to think about what it all means. Because you come with a title and a throne and a whole life planned out for you. That's insane for me to try and take in. And second of all, more than anyone here, I know that you hold your cards close to your chest. A confession like that must be practically painful for you."

I nodded. "Not that I'm mad that I like you . . . except that I kind of am."

He laughed. "It is rather infuriating."

"But I need to know, now, before we go any further, do you feel anything like that for me? Even the smallest glimmer of something? Because if not, I have to make plans."

"And if I do?"

I lifted my arms and let them flop down to my sides again. "Then I still have to make plans, but they'll be different."

He sighed heavily. "Turns out you matter to me, too. And I wouldn't have thought about it except for my designs lately."

"Uh . . . how romantic?"

He laughed. "No, really, it kind of is. Usually I get excited about designing skyscrapers and homeless shelters, things that someone might remember, or might help people. But the other day I found myself designing you a summerhouse, a miniature palace, maybe something with a vineyard. This morning I got an idea for a beach house."

I gasped. "I've always wanted a beach house!"

"Not that we'd ever get to use it with you running the world and all."

"It's a sweet thought all the same."

He shrugged. "It just seems like everything I want to make lately is something for you."

"That means a lot. I know how important your work is to you."

"It's not really my work. Something that I care about is all."

"Okay, then. How about for now we just add this to that pile? This is something we care about, and we both know it, and we'll watch it and see what happens."

"That's fair. I don't want to discourage you at all, but it feels too soon to call this love."

"Absolutely!" I agreed. "It's too soon, and that's too big."

"Too busy."

"Too scary."

He laughed. "On par with being dethroned?"

"At least!"

"Wow. Okay." He continued to smile, probably considering the unlikelihood of us falling for each other himself. "So, what now?"

"I continue the Selection, I think. I don't want to hurt your feelings, but I have to keep going. I have to be certain."

He nodded. "I wouldn't want you if you weren't."

"Thank you, sir."

We stood there, the sound of the wind in the grass the only noise.

He cleared his throat. "I think we need food."

"As long as I don't have to cook it."

He threw his arm around my shoulder as we turned back to the palace. It felt like a very boyfriendish thing to do. "But we did so great last time."

"All I learned about was butter."

"Then you know everything."

In the morning I headed straight down to the hospital wing, desperate to see Mom's face. Even if she was asleep, I just needed to be reminded she was alive and healing. But when I cracked open the door this time, she was sitting up, wide awake . . . and Dad was asleep. Smiling, she held up a finger to her lips. With her other hand she traced gentle lines through his hair as he lay spilled out of his chair and onto her bed, one arm beneath his head and the other across her lap.

I quietly walked to the other side of the bed to kiss her cheek.

"I keep waking up in the night," she whispered, giving me a little squeeze. "All these tubes and things are bothering me. And every time, he's awake, watching me. It does me good to see him sleep."

"Me, too. He's been looking a little rough."

She smiled. "Eh. I've seen him worse. He'll make it through this, too."

"Have the doctors checked on you yet?"

She shook her head. "I asked them to come again once he's rested a little. I'll get back to my room soon enough."

Of course. Of course the woman who just had a heart attack could spare getting herself to a more comfortable place so her husband could take a nap. Seriously, even if I did find someone, could it ever compare to them?

"How are you doing? Is everyone being helpful?" Mom continued to run her hand through Dad's hair.

"I fired Coddly. I don't think I told you yesterday."

She stilled, staring intently. "What? Why?"

"Oh, no big deal. He just wanted to go to war."

She covered her mouth, trying not to laugh at how cavalierly I discussed invasion. A second later she stopped smiling at all and moved both of her hands to her chest.

"Mom?" I asked too loudly. Dad's head instantly shot up.

"Darling? What's wrong?"

Mom shook her head. "It's just the stitches. I'm fine."

Dad settled back into his seat but sat up, done with sleep

for the moment. Mom tried to start up the conversation again, doing anything to take the focus off herself.

"How about the Selection? How are things going there?"

I paused. "Umm, okay, I think. I haven't had a lot of time to spend with the boys, but I'm going to work on that. Especially since there's a *Report* coming up."

"You know, honey, no one would fault you for calling it off. You've been through a lot this last week, and you're acting as regent. I'm not sure you should be trying to balance all this."

"They are very nice boys," Dad offered, "but if it's taking too much of your focus . . ."

I sighed. "I think we need to stop dancing around the fact that I am not the most beloved member of this family. At least not to the general public. You say no one would fault me, but I feel very confident they would." Mom and Dad shared a look, seeming to want to refute this but not wanting to lie at the same time. "If I'm going to be queen one day, I need to win the people over."

"And you think finding a husband is the way to accomplish that?" Mom asked suspiciously.

"Yes. It's all about their perception of me. They think I'm too cold. The most absolute way to refute that would be to get married. They think I'm too masculine. The most absolute way to refute that is to be a bride."

"I don't know. I'm still very hesitant about you continuing."

"Need I remind you that this Selection was your idea?"

She sighed.

"Listen to your daughter," Dad said. "Very smart girl. Gets it from me."

"Don't you want some more sleep?" she asked flatly.

"No, I'm feeling very refreshed," he said. I wasn't sure if it was because he wanted to continue the conversation or if he felt he needed to keep his attention on Mom. Either way, he was clearly lying.

"Dad, you look like death punched you in the face."

"You must get that from me, too."

"Dad!"

He laughed, and Mom did, too, her hand going back to put pressure on her chest.

"Look! Your terrible jokes are now life threatening. You have to stop them."

He shared a smile with Mom. "Go do what you need to do, Eadlyn. We will support you in whatever way we can."

"Thank you. Both of you, please get some rest."

"Ugh, she's so bossy," Mom lamented.

Dad nodded. "I know. Who does she think she is?"

I looked back at them one last time. Dad gave me a wink. No matter who was against me today, at least I had them.

I left them and strode upstairs to the office, shocked to find a beautiful bouquet of flowers on my desk.

"Someone thinks you're doing a good job, huh?" Neena remarked.

"Or they think I'll die from the stress and wanted to beat everyone to the punch," I joked, not sure I wanted to admit how happily surprised I was.

"Lighten up. You've been doing great." But Neena's eyes weren't even on me. They had zoomed in on the card.

I tucked it close to my chest as she whined, and lifted the note just enough so I could read it.

You looked a little down when we parted the other day. Wanted today to start on a happier note. I'm here for you.—Marid

I smiled and passed it to Neena, who sighed before turning back to look at the huge bouquet.

"Who are those from?" General Leger asked, coming in the door.

"Marid Illéa," I replied.

"I heard he stopped by. Was he just bringing gifts or did he need something?" the general asked, skepticism painting his tone.

"Oddly enough, he was making sure I didn't need something. He offered to give me a helping hand with the public. He knows a lot more about people living their lives in the wake of the castes than I do."

General Leger joined me beside the table and stared at the extravagant arrangement. "I don't know. Things didn't exactly end well between your family and his."

"I remember. Vividly. But it might be a good thing to learn a little now for when my time comes."

The general smiled at me, his face softening. "It's already

here, Your Highness. Be careful who you trust, okay?"

"Yes, sir."

Neena was still acting swoony. "Someone needs to tell Mark to step up. I just got a huge promotion. Where are my flowers?"

"Maybe he's planning to deliver them in person. Much more romantic," I said.

"Pssh! The way that boy works?" she said skeptically. "If everyone in the palace died and I somehow became queen, he probably still couldn't get time off. He's always so busy."

Though she was trying to joke, I could sense her sadness. "But he loves it, right?"

"Oh, yes, he likes his research. It's just hard that he's so busy, and that he's far away."

I didn't know what else to say on the subject, so I turned the conversation back to my gift. "They're a bit much, though, don't you think?"

"I think they're perfect."

I shook my head. "Either way, these should probably be moved somewhere else."

"Don't you want to look at them?" Neena questioned even as she went to grab the vase.

"No. I need the desk space."

She shrugged and carefully lifted the arrangement to take it into the parlor. I sat down at the desk, trying to concentrate. I had to focus if I was going to win my people over. And that was what I had to do—Ahren had said so.

"Wait!" My voice was a little louder than I intended, and

Neena started. "Put them back where they were."

She made a face at me but brought them back all the same. "What made you change your mind?"

I looked up at the bouquet and ran my fingers across a few of the low-hanging petals. "I just remembered I could lead and still like flowers."

CHAPTER 7

By THE TIME DINNER ROLLED around, I was very concerned that I might fall asleep on my plate. There was a chance no one would mind if I skipped it. Meals had generally been quiet unless I worked to make them otherwise. But when I came downstairs and saw Grandma Singer flinging her bag at a butler, I knew tonight was going to be anything but dull.

"Don't you tell me I can't come at such an hour!" She shook her wrinkled fist, and I bit my lips to hold in the laughter.

"I wasn't, ma'am," the guard replied, his voice anxious. "I just said it was getting late in the day."

"The queen will want to see me!"

Grandma Singer was a fearsome creature. If we ever did have a war under my rule, my plan was to send her to the front lines. She'd come home holding the enemy by his ear within a week.

I walked into the foyer. "Grandma."

She instantly turned from the guard, her face melting into the sweetest expression. "Oh, there's my precious girl. The TV doesn't do you justice—you're so lovely!"

I bent so she could kiss me on both cheeks. "Thanks . . . I think."

"Where is your mother? I've been wanting to come over, but May insisted I stay out of the way."

"She's doing much better now. I can take you to her, but wouldn't you like to eat first and recover from your trip?" I gestured toward the dining hall.

Grandma had lived in the palace when I was younger, but after years of Mom trying to take care of her, she finally up and left. Her "long journey" was really only an hour across town, but it might as well be from the other side of Illéa for how she behaved about it.

"Now, that would be wonderful," she said, coming beside me. "See, that's how you treat your elders. There's some respect." Her eyes darted back to the poor guard, who stood there stupefied, with her bag in his hands.

"Thank you, Officer Farrow. Please take that to the guest suite on the third floor overlooking the gardens."

He bowed and left as we made our way into the room. A few of the boys were already waiting, and their eyebrows raised at the sight of the queen mother. Fox strode up immediately to introduce himself.

"Ms. Singer, such a pleasure to meet you," he said, extending his hand.

"Now, he's a cute one, Eady. Look at this face." Grandma grabbed his chin, and he laughed through her grip.

"Yes, Grandma, I know. Part of why he's still here." I mouthed an apology, but Fox shook his head, positively beaming over her approval.

Gunner, Hale, and Henri all came over to meet her, and I took the chance to speak quietly to Erik.

"Are you busy tomorrow?"

He squinted. "I don't think so. Why?"

"Just planning a little something with Henri."

"Oh," he said, shaking his head as if that should have been obvious. "No, we'll both be free."

"Okay. Don't tell," I insisted.

"Of course not."

"What?" Grandma shouted. "Say that again?"

Erik hopped over, bowing.

"So sorry, ma'am. Sir Henri was born in Swendway and only speaks Finnish. I'm his translator. He says he's very pleased to meet you."

"Oh, that's right, that's right." Grandma took Henri's hand. "IT'S NICE TO MEET YOU, TOO!"

I moved her toward the head table. "He's not deaf, Grandma."

"Well," she said, as if that was enough of an explanation.

"Have you talked to Uncle Gerad?"

"Gerad wants to be here, but he's working on a time-sensitive project. You know I never understand a word he says." Grandma waved her arm in the air as if she was slapping away the elaborate words he used. "I heard from Kota, too. He's not sure if he should stop by or not. Your mother and him, they've tried over the years, but they just can't seem to be civil. He's gotten better, though. I think it's that wife of his."

I ushered her around the table, and she took my seat. Even though it wasn't permanent, taking Dad's empty place next to her felt strange. So much had been entrusted to me, yet I felt like I'd stolen something of his.

"Aunt Leah does sound like a rather calming person," I agreed. "I guess those things matter, balancing each other out."

The butlers rushed some soup in front of Grandma, knowing how short her patience was. I smiled as she dug in.

"Worked for your grandpa and me. Your parents, too."

Ignoring my own bowl, I rested my chin on my hand. "What was Grandpa like?"

"Good. Very good. He always wanted to do what was right. He was slower to get upset than I was and didn't let things get him down. I wish you could have known him."

"Me, too."

I let her eat and found my eyes wandering around the room. Kile was my opposite in that he was humble where I was proud. Henri was my opposite in that he saw everything as a joy where I focused on the challenge. Ean, Fox, Gunner . . . there was an element in each of them that would fall on the other side of my spectrum.

"Is the French girl like that for Ahren?" Grandma asked with no attempt to hide her disdain.

I considered this. "No, actually. It's like they're two halves of the same heart in different bodies." My eyes welled. I was so tired, and I missed him so much. "I can't begin to tell you how much he loves her."

She grumbled. "Enough to leave."

I exhaled slowly. "Exactly, Grandma. It hurt him so much to be apart from her that he would endure the pain of leaving his family, his home, and his country, not even knowing how that would all be received, just to be with her."

She recognized the sadness in my voice and reached out her hand to mine.

"You all right, honey?"

I pulled myself together. "Of course. A little tired is all. I should go rest." Just then Kaden and Osten came running in, giving me a perfect escape. "The boys will take you to Mom."

She shrieked in delight. "My boys!"

I backed away while she was distracted, walking quietly down the side of the room until I got to Henri.

I tapped him on his shoulder, and he looked up from his meal, that ever-present smile on his face. "Hello today!"

I chuckled. "Would you like to join me for lunch tomorrow?"

I waited for Erik to jump in, but Henri held up a hand, concentrating. "Tomorrow, lunch?" he asked.

"Yes."

"Good, good! Yes!"

I smiled. "See you then."

I left the room, peeking back to see Henri clutching Erik by the shoulder, elated by the invitation. He seemed so pleased to have made it through the interaction without needing a translation, too. Erik nodded at Henri, pleased for his friend . . . but I'd seen him smile brighter than that before.

I looked at the clock. Ten after midnight. If I fell asleep right now, I could get about five hours of sleep.

Ten minutes later it was clear that wasn't going to happen. I used to be so good at shutting off my mind for the day, but now it seemed like every task I was halfway through stayed with me until it was done, not caring if I was well rested enough to tackle it.

I slipped on my robe, combed my fingers through my hair, and stepped barefoot into the hallway. Perhaps if I went to the office I could do some work and appease my brain, and then I could get back to bed. But if I was going to do that, I needed coffee.

It was too late for any maids to be on duty, so I headed to the kitchen. It seemed it was never empty down there, and I was sure someone would help me. Rounding the landing on the second floor, I leaped back, startled by the figure coming right at me.

"Oh!" Erik said, suddenly realizing someone was in his path.

I pulled my robe a little tighter, though I was fully covered, and swept back my hair, hoping to seem less surprised than I had been.

He backed up, fidgeted with his hands a second, and then bowed abruptly. It was such a rushed, sloppy gesture that I couldn't help but laugh.

He smiled a little himself, shaking his head at the silliness of the moment. He, too, was in his pajamas—striped-blue pants and a plain cotton shirt—and wandering the palace in bare feet.

"What in the world are you doing up at this hour?" I asked.

"Henri has been working especially hard on his English since you announced the Elite. And with a date tomorrow, he wanted to be extra prepared. We only quit for the day a few minutes ago, and I was heading to the kitchen for some tea and honey. Honey is supposed to make you sleep well." He said all this in a low, hurried voice, as if he was worried he might bore me.

"Is it? I might have to try that tomorrow. I was actually just going to the kitchen for coffee."

"Your Highness, I feel you're a very bright woman, so it pains me to tell you that coffee will not help you sleep. Not at all."

I giggled. "No, I know. I was going to get some work done. I haven't been sleeping, so I thought I might as well be useful."

"I'm pretty sure you're always useful. Even when you sleep."

I ducked my head, moving around the banister, and he followed me down the steps. All I could think of was how drab he had seemed that first day, a grayed-out shadow of a person. I knew now his plainness was his shield, hiding how smart, thoughtful, and funny he was. Though I still didn't understand the choice, I knew there was more to him than he let most people see.

"How is Henri doing? With the English lessons?"

He shrugged and tucked his hands behind his back. "Good. Not great. What I told you before is still very true; it would be a long time before you could communicate on your own. But he cares so much, he's been trying harder than ever." He nodded to himself as if assessing their work in his head. "Forgive me—I should have asked. How are your parents? I heard your mother is awake and recovering."

"She is, thank you. She was supposed to move back to her room today, but there was something funny about her oxygen levels so they kept her in the hospital wing one more night for good measure. And Dad is still sleeping in a cot by her bed."

Erik grinned. "It makes the idea of 'in sickness and in health' much more real to see it play out in front of you."

I nodded. "Honestly, sometimes it's intimidating to watch

them. Finding anything close to what they have seems impossible."

He smirked. "There's no way to know everything about someone else's relationship, even your parents'. Sometimes especially your parents'," he added, as if he'd thought about this before, perhaps about his own family. "I guarantee you—he's given a terrible Christmas present at least once and has earned himself a day of silence for it."

"Highly unlikely."

Erik was unfazed. "You have to embrace the idea of imperfection, even in the thing that is most perfect for you. Your brother whisked away a girl and got married in a whirlwind and could be discovering right now that she snores so loudly, he can't even sleep."

I covered my mouth, but not fast enough to smother the laugh that escaped. Something about the image of poor Ahren with pillows slammed over his ears really got me.

"It's very possible," he added, looking quite pleased to have made me smile.

"You've ruined my image of Camille! How am I supposed to keep a straight face the next time I see her?"

"Don't," he said simply. "Just laugh. Your impression of everyone is probably wrong in some way."

Shaking my head, I sighed. "I'm sure you're right. Which makes everything I do that much harder."

"Like the Selection?"

"There are moments when a room full of politicians seems easier to manage than six boys. For everything I've learned so far, there must be a dozen things I've missed."

"Relying heavily on gut instincts then?"

"Very heavily."

"Well, they've been spot-on about Henri. He's as nice as he seems. You must have already known that, though, to keep him in the final pool." I noticed something off about his tone as he spoke, like this was a disappointing thing to admit.

I clasped my hands together, only just then realizing that we'd moved well past the kitchen. I supposed I could always go back for coffee if I still wanted a cup.

"This whole situation has been a hard one to navigate. I wasn't supposed to have a Selection. In the past, princesses were married off for international relations, but my parents promised they'd never do that to me. So to find myself with a roomful of boys and be expected to choose a lifelong partner from them . . . it's scary. All I have to go on are a handful of impressions, and a hope that no one is deceiving me."

I risked a glance at him, and he was attentive, his expression downcast. "That sounds incredibly frightening," he said slowly. "I'm surprised it's worked so well in the past. I don't want to sound rude, but it does seem a bit unfair."

I nodded. "That's exactly what I said when the idea was presented to me. But they insisted that I try, so . . ."

"So . . . this wasn't your idea?"

I froze.

"Did you even want it to happen?"

There's a chill that runs down your back when you realize

you've been caught in a lie. And it was scary, because this had already been hinted at in the papers, guessed at by plenty of people.

"Erik, this needs to stay between us," I said quietly, the words coming out more like a request than a command. "I admit, in the beginning, I wanted nothing to do with the Selection. But now . . ."

"Now you're in love?" he asked, his tone both curious and melancholy.

I laughed once. "I'm a lot of things. Infatuated, frightened, desperate, hopeful. It'd be nice to add 'in love' to the list." I thought of Kile and our conversation in the garden. *Love* was still too big a word for that, and none of what I'd said to Kile felt appropriate to share with Erik. "Sometimes I think I'm close, but right now, the Selection is something I need to finish. For a lot of reasons. A lot of people, too."

"I certainly hope you're one of them."

"I am," I promised. "Just maybe not in the way people would think."

He didn't answer. He merely walked along, taking in my words.

"You can't repeat any of that, not to anyone. I can't believe I said those things to you. If this Selection seems like it was a joke or fake in any way—"

He held up a hand. "You don't have to worry about me. I'd never break your confidence. I assume it's not an easy thing to acquire in the first place, and I'd hate to waste it."

I smiled. "Well, you more than earned it. You've kept secrets for me already, and pulled me out of the middle of a fight, and brought me a flower when you didn't have to."

"It was only a dandelion."

"Perspective," I reminded him, and he grinned at his words coming back to stare him in the face. "All I'm saying is, you've done a lot for me without being under any obligation to do so. You've earned my trust."

"Good," he said plainly. "Because I'm here for you, anything you need, any time you need it."

The sincerity in his voice was so painfully clear that I was drawn to a standstill. Erik's eyes were clear and blue, a stark contrast to his dark hair. Maybe that was why they stood out so brilliantly in the moment.

"Really?" I asked, though I had no reason to doubt his words.

"Of course," he replied. "You're going to be my sovereign. It's a privilege to serve you."

I cleared my throat. "Yes. Right. Thank you. It's a comfort knowing there are at least a handful of people I don't have to break my back to win over."

His smile was kind, and I reminded myself that this was a victory, to have someone like him on my side.

"If you'll excuse me," I said, stepping away, "I really ought to try to sleep."

He bowed. "Of course. I know I'm meant to be at Henri's

disposal, but please let me know if there's anything else I can do to help you."

I smiled, not answering, and strode back to my room, my back as straight as an arrow.

CHAPTER 8

"For the *Report* tonight, the focus will be on you." Lady Brice was pacing in front of my desk. It was comforting to watch her elegant steps as she thought everything through. Dad was like that sometimes. He'd make me walk the garden with him while he was trying to unravel a mess.

"I know I don't have much experience doing this alone, but Gavril will be there to help. And I have an idea how to address my progress with the Selection."

"Good. It's about time you brought something to the table," she teased. "Speaking of the Selection, there's something else. I'm trying to decide if it's worth addressing."

I squinted. "What's going on?"

"Well," she started. "Marid Illéa was on another radio program yesterday. We have a recording if you'd like to hear it, but basically, it's gotten out that he's visited the palace and that he sent you flowers."

"So?"

"So he was asked if that meant anything."

I stared at her. "But I'm in the middle of a Selection. How . . . ?"

"He said the same thing, but also said he regretted falling out of touch with you and how beautiful and intelligent you grew up to be." She raised an eyebrow as I felt my insides flutter a little.

"He said that?"

She nodded.

"Why are we bringing this up?" I tried to even my breaths.

"You need to be aware that you two have been linked in the press. And it could do one of two things: undermine your Selection to the point that it seems you don't care about it or—"

"How could it undermine it?"

"Well, if it seems like you're abandoning your suitors for him . . ."

"Got it. What's the second thing?"

"It could offer up another suitor, if you're not opposed."

I laughed. "I'm confident the rules of the Selection are pretty binding. I don't think I could simply quit it for someone else, could I?"

She shrugged. "He's pretty popular."

"Are you advising me to consider him?"

"No. I'm advising you to be aware that this has become

public, and you need to be conscious of how you interact with him. And with the Elite."

"I can do that. Especially since I've hardly interacted with him. I don't want to do anything that might undermine this process. I've already accidentally done that so many times, and I want the people to know this matters to me. I've done nothing to encourage Marid, and I don't think it's worth addressing on the *Report*."

"Agreed."

"Good." Only for me would a generous act of kindness be twisted into something scandalous.

"And, now don't take this the wrong way, but what are you wearing tonight?"

I looked down at myself. "I have no idea. I've hardly been able to dress myself."

She studied my clothes. "This will seem like an insult, but trust me when I say that's not how it's intended. I think you need to step it up a little. While the clothes you've chosen or designed in the past have been beautiful, it's time we move on from playing with your fashion to using it as a means of backing up your words."

It felt like a stab to the gut, thinking of undoing this image I'd made just for me and turning it into something for other people. "I get that. What are you thinking?"

She crossed her arms, thinking. "You could borrow one of your mother's dresses?"

I looked at the clock. "If I go now, I can pick something.

But Neena's the only one who could alter it quickly enough, and she needs to finish my schedule for next week. And I have a lunch date."

She clasped her hands together. "Ohhhhh."

"Seriously? As if it wasn't bad enough to have my grandmother tell Fox how cute he is."

Lady Brice wrapped her arms around herself and laughed. "Did she really?"

"There's no stopping that woman."

"It must run in the family. Hurry. Go pick a dress."

"Okay. Send for Hale. I'm sure he's just as skilled as Neena, and I guess we'll find out how fast he is. And make a bullet point list for me for tonight. I'm terrified I'm going to blank."

"I'm on it."

I hurried into the hallway, hoping Mom hadn't been released from the hospital wing yet because I was going to feel wholly awful if I bothered her by looking for a dress in her room. No more than two steps out the door, I saw Gunner waiting for me. He popped off the bench immediately and bowed.

"Hi. Is everything all right?" I asked, coming over.

"Yeah," he said. "Well, except that I'm probably about to do something so incredibly stupid that I can feel my heartbeat banging in my feet."

"Oh, please don't. I've had enough stupid to last a lifetime."

He chuckled. "No, it's not like that. I just . . . I wanted to ask you for something."

I raised my eyebrows, proceeding with caution. "All right. You have two minutes."

He gulped loudly. "Okay, wow. So I'm really flattered that you kept me in the top six. It made me feel like I did something right, though I'm still clueless as to what that was."

I shrugged. "Your poem made me laugh. Laughter is important."

He smiled. "I agree, but it kind of proves my point." He fidgeted with his hands. "It's just, this far in, with you so busy and with me never having had one-on-one time with you, I was wondering how good my chances are."

"It's a fair question. But I can't really answer it right now. I have so much to figure out."

"Exactly," he replied enthusiastically. "So I am going to ask for something ridiculous. Could I kiss you?"

I stepped back. "Excuse me?"

"We don't have to do this if you don't want to. But I think a kiss can say a lot. I think one kiss would be enough for you to know if it's worth me pursing you or you pursuing me."

There was something sweet about his request, like even though a picture of me kissing Kile had been plastered across the country, he still didn't think it was a given that I'd just go and kiss anyone. And that he'd learned enough from Jack's expulsion to move with care. That alone made me want to give him what he was asking for. But to do this, to potentially lose a final suitor without even trying to know him better? It felt foolish.

"You could be a prince. You could have more money than

you knew what to do with, be so famous people who don't even have televisions would know your face. Are you willing to bet all of that on one kiss?"

"I'm willing to bet your happiness and mine on it."

I inhaled, thinking. "Okay."

"Yes?"

"Yes."

Once the surprise wore off, Gunner placed his hand on my waist. He lowered his face to mine, stopping momentarily to laugh.

"This is a bit surreal."

"I'm waiting, sir."

He smiled just before our lips touched. There were plenty of good things about the kiss. His mouth wasn't rigid, and he didn't try to stick his tongue down my throat. He also smelled pretty good, though not like cinnamon or flowers or anything recognizable. Overall, I would say not bad.

But then, the fact that I could make that assessment as it was going on . . .

Gunner pulled away, pressed his lips together, and considered.

"No, right?"

He shook his head. "I don't think so. Not that it was bad!"

"It just wasn't that good."

"Exactly." His stance shifted in relief. "Thank you so much for this experience, but I think it's time for me to head home."

I smiled. "You sure? You're welcome to stay for the *Report*, go home in the morning."

"Nah." He smiled bashfully. "I think if I stayed, I'd try to talk myself back into it. You might be the most beautiful girl I'll ever meet, but . . . I don't think you're the girl for me. I'd hate to find a reason why you could be when I've been trying to tell myself for a while that it was unlikely."

I held out my hand. "I respect that. Best of luck to you, sir."

Gunner shook my hand. "And to you, Your Highness."

As Gunner made his way to the stairwell, I saw a butler escorting Hale toward Mom's room. I waved him over, though his eyes were on my dismissed suitor as they passed.

"What was Gunner doing up here?" he asked.

"Making a choice. Come with me. I need your hands."

CHAPTER 9

I came out of Mom's closet wearing our top pick, pressing it to my chest to save my modesty. "Thank you for doing this," I said as Hale went to work, pulling at seams and pinning them in place.

"Are you kidding? I'm helping dress my future queen right now. I'm over the moon." He pulled some more, watching the way the fabric reacted in the mirror. "Of course, it's not the same as building you a gown from scratch, but this will be an impressive addition to my resume."

I chuckled. "I just feel bad you have to give up your afternoon for this."

"Well, it gets kind of boring in the Men's Parlor. I'm sure if I ask Kile, he'll come and sit with me while I work. Or Ean, maybe."

"Ean," I said, shocked. "It's hard to imagine him willingly

joining anyone anywhere."

Hale smiled. "Yeah. I think he's finally getting used to us. He talks to me sometimes, and to Erik. Probably because he's not competition."

"That makes sense. Ean seems like the 'not here to make friends' type, but I don't think anyone could go through this without getting close to someone. It's too hard. As difficult as it is for me, I know it's just as bad for you all."

"We definitely get the better end of the deal though," he said, winking at my reflection.

I tilted my head. "I don't know about that. The more I think about it, the sadder I get about having to send all but one of you away. I'll miss having you here."

"Have you considered a harem?" he said, deadpan.

I bent over in laughter and was rewarded with a pin stabbing my waist. "Ow!"

"Sorry! I shouldn't joke when there are needles around." He walked in front of me, and I held still, watching his eyes, recognizing the analytical gaze, knowing I did the same thing myself to designs and proposals and sometimes even to people. "I think we need to streamline this a little. Are you sure this is absolutely okay with the queen? Because some of these cuts I can't undo."

"Don't worry. You have full permission to tweak in any way you deem necessary."

"That makes me feel so important."

"Well, you are. You're helping me look like a leader tonight. It takes a thousand little things to make this role work, so I owe you one. Or two. At least two."

"You all right?"

I looked up, not realizing how somber I'd gotten. "Yes. It's just a lot to deal with sometimes. I'm trying to hold it together, that's all."

Hale pulled a pin from the pile the maid had left us and held it up for me. "Use this next time you feel like things are falling apart. It'll help, I promise."

Slowly I took it, spinning it between my finger and thumb, and, at least for a moment, I believed it was true.

Henri was right on time, rushing into the parlor as if he'd been dying to run down for the last fifteen minutes. He bypassed ceremony as he held my hands and kissed my cheek, making me laugh.

"Hello today!"

I smiled. "Hello, Henri."

Over Henri's shoulder, Erik bowed, and I gave him a nod.

I took Henri's arm and led him to the table, laid with two settings fairly close together and a third slightly distanced.

"Here," Henri said, pulling out my chair.

Once I was seated, he eagerly ran around the table to sit across from me . . . and the conversation drew to an abrupt halt. I pulled the cover off my plate so they would know they could do the same, and after a few silent bites, I worked to bridge the gap.

"How's your family?" I asked. "And your sister?"

"*Miten on* Annika?" he said, turning to Erik for confirmation. He nodded, and Henri returned to me, delighted. "Good. She very good. We miss."

I gave him a sad look and nodded. "I understand completely. You have no idea how much I wish Ahren was here."

He kept his expression calm but leaned over to Erik, who muttered a translation of my answer as quickly as he could.

"Your mom? Is good?" Henri said, trying so hard.

"Yes, thank goodness. Heading back to her room right now and recovering nicely."

Once again Erik came to our rescue. We went back and forth in the same way for a few more minutes, and even with all the effort he'd been putting into learning English, Henri was as lost as I was. I hated this. It was too impersonal. It was one thing to need a translator for a visiting dignitary, but for someone who was in my home daily, it felt like too much. Even if Henri's time in the palace was short-lived, I really wanted to be able to speak with him, just him, at least from time to time.

"Erik, how does Henri do with the other Elite? Do they all speak through you?"

He sat taller, taking this in. "Mostly. Hale and Kile have picked up a few words."

"And the others?"

He pursed his lips, looking guilty, as if he was worried he'd sully the reputation of the others. "Gunner has been marginally interested, as is Fox, but they don't appear to want to take on the challenge. It's a lot of work. And Ean will speak with me but doesn't really try to speak with Henri."

I let out a long sigh, several thoughts flitting through my

head. "Would you be up to giving us all a little Finnish lesson tomorrow morning?"

Erik raised his eyebrows. "Really?"

"Absolutely. It seems unfair that Henri has to do all the work." As I said his name, Henri's eyes darted over to me. He was certainly following our conversation in his own way, but I was excited for him to discover exactly where this was going.

Erik spoke swiftly in Finnish, and Henri's eyes lit up.

"I speak, too? I speaking?" he asked as if this was going to be a party instead of a lesson.

"Of course," I said, and Henri sat there, completely beside himself, the gears already turning in his head.

"I think you just made his day," Erik commented.

"I'm upset I didn't think of it sooner. It will make things easier on everyone."

"I hope so. But I'm still going to focus on the English lessons. I'm hoping to avoid any more appearances on the *Report*."

I made a face. "It wasn't that bad."

"It was awful!" After shaking his head, he pointed his fork at me. "My mom will not stop talking about it. 'You look so good! Why didn't you smile more?' I swear, it's maddening."

"You're blaming me?" I asked, feigning indignation.

"Forever. Forever I am blaming you! I don't like being on camera." He shuddered. I was glad he didn't actually seem angry, though I could sense how serious he was about it.

I laughed, and he looked down bashfully at his plate as he smiled. It was then I realized Henri was stuck watching me chat with his translator while I was supposed to be on a date with him.

"You know, Henri, maybe we could do a full Swendish immersion experience, and you could teach everyone to make that soup you were talking about."

Erik translated, and once again Henri was jubilant. *"Kala-keitto!"* he exclaimed.

There were things I was curious about with Henri. I wanted to know more about his family, particularly his sister. And I wanted to know if he was at peace with the idea of living here and working beside me, or if it worried him that we could have moments like the parade all over again and he'd be stuck trying to protect me from angry masses for the rest of his life. I wanted to ask him about that kiss in the kitchen, if he'd thought about it much or dismissed it as a lapse of judgment on one or both our parts.

But until I could ask him those things without having to ask Erik, too, there was no way I'd be able to.

CHAPTER 10

THE DRESS WAS RED. MOM hadn't worn it in years, which was one of the reasons I chose it. Hale trimmed the long lace sleeves up to my elbows and pulled a few of the layers from beneath the gown so it wasn't quite as full. He was right about some of this being irreversible, but he'd handled it all so tastefully that even if Mom eventually wanted it back, she'd probably be thrilled with the alterations.

Eloise helped me do my hair, and it looked so smart, with braids leading back to a modest bun. I chose a tiara with rubies in it, and I looked like I was on fire.

It was beautiful, really. I knew that, and I was thankful for all the hands that had gone into making me look like someone who could be trusted with the decisions that had to be made on behalf of the country. It just felt old, older than I truly was, though maybe closer to the age I should behave.

Sighing, I came to terms with the dress. This was who I had to be for now.

I was tugging at my seams in the studio when Josie came up to talk to me. "That dress is amazing," she praised, unable to keep her fingers off the layers of satin.

I kept straightening. "It's my mother's."

"I'm sorry about all that, by the way," she said quietly. "Don't think I've told you yet."

I swallowed. "Thank you, Josie. That means a lot."

"You know, since everything's been so serious, it might be a good idea to have a party."

I huffed out an almost laugh. "I'm a little busy for that. Maybe once things settle down."

"I could plan it! Just let me talk to a few maids, and we could pull something together in a week."

I turned from the mirror. "Like I said, maybe one day, but not now." I moved away, trying to focus.

She trailed me across the room, insistent. "But why? Shouldn't you be celebrating? I mean, you're practically the queen, so—"

I spun on her, enraged. "But I am *not* the queen. That title belongs to my mother, who nearly *died*. That you so casually brush over that fact makes the condolences you just gave me meaningless. What don't you get, Josie? Do you think this job is nothing but dresses and galas?"

She stood there, stunned. I watched her eyes dart around the room, checking to see if anyone was watching our interaction. I didn't want to humiliate her. In a way, I understood her. There might have been a time when nothing brought me more joy than a reason to start a guest list, a time when I thought this role was nothing more than dresses and galas myself. . . .

I sighed. "I'm not trying to insult you. But it would be inappropriate to throw a party when my mother is still recuperating. Please, what I need from you tonight is some level of understanding, which I realize may be too much, considering our history. Still, for my sanity, I beg you, just try to consider what it's like to be in my shoes."

She sulked. "That's all I've ever wanted. Of course that only matters to you when it's convenient."

I wanted to rip her head off. What part about my life right now did she think was convenient? But I had a broadcast to think about.

"Excuse me?" I called to a passing maid. "Please escort Miss Josie to her room. Her attitude tonight is unsettling, and I need to concentrate."

"Yes, Your Highness." The maid turned cheerfully to Josie, not worried about our personal issues and ready to do her job.

Josie huffed. "I hate you."

I pointed to the door. "Yes, and you can do that from your room just as well as from here."

Without waiting to see if she obeyed, I made my way to my seat. I'd never seen it set up this way: the Elite on one side and a single chair on the other.

As I was staring at the sad, lonely seat, Kile sidled up to me.

"What was that with Josie?"

I smiled and batted my eyes. "Nothing, sweetheart. Just making me seriously doubt how much I want her as an in-law."

"Still too soon."

I laughed. "No, we had a . . . disagreement. And I feel kind of bad, because I understand her. I just wish she could understand *me*."

"That might be hard for Josie. She's only aware of herself. Also, have you seen Gunner?"

I squinted. "He left this afternoon. Didn't he say good-bye?"

Kile shook his head.

I walked over to the other boys, who all sat up straighter as I approached. "Did Gunner say good-bye to any of you?"

The others shook their heads in confusion as Fox cleared his throat. "He stopped by to see me. Gunner's a bit sentimental, and he didn't have it in him to go through a long farewell. He just said this wasn't right for him and that he had your approval to go."

"He did. We parted on very good terms."

Fox nodded. "I think he thought he'd lose his resolve if he stuck around. He asked me to pass on to everyone how much he would miss you." He smiled. "Really nice guy."

"He was. But take his words to heart," I pleaded, looking at each of their faces. "This is about your futures as well. Don't stay for something that you might not be able to handle."

Kile nodded, looking suddenly pensive. Hale gave me a bright smile. Ean was impassive as ever, and Henri was taking in Erik's translation, looking confused.

Certainly I'd spend the rest of my evening overanalyzing their expressions, but for now, we had a show to put on.

"Hale," I whispered, pointing to the gown. "Thank you."

"Beautiful," he mouthed. I knew he meant it, and I tried to hold myself taller. I wanted to do this dress justice tonight.

The cameras went on, and I greeted the country as honestly as I could.

"Let me begin with the news you're most eager to hear. My mother is doing well. As I speak, she is healing in her room, with my father by her side." I tried to stop focusing on how I was standing or what I should do with my hands. Instead I thought of my parents, no doubt watching this in pajamas with doctor-approved snacks by their sides. And when I pictured that, I smiled. "We all know that their love story may be the truest one ever told. Though it has been no small task to step into my father's role.

"My brother, Ahren, now the prince consort of France, is also a testament to the power of the deepest love. From what I understand, he is settling into his new position very well and is already very happy to be a husband." My smile crept through again. "None of this surprises me. His devotion to Princess Camille over both time and distance has been constant and strong, and I can only imagine his happiness at getting to be beside her every moment.

"As for the country at large"—I glanced at my notes, though I hated to do it—"some of the disquiet we've been experiencing has diminished over the last few weeks." In one way that was absolutely true, but as far as disquiet related to me, my nose ought to be growing as I spoke. "Taking into account how much work my father has put into the cause of peace abroad, the thought that we could finally be achieving a greater peace at home brings me extraordinary joy."

I hit on everything I was supposed to—the budget proposal, the upcoming start to the drilling project, and the change in the advisory board, which made a few people in the room squirm—and when it was all done, I searched the crowd for a few important faces. Lady Brice gave me a big nod, as did General Leger. I saw Grandma fidgeting, impatient with the lengthy announcements, and likely only holding on so she could hear the boys speak. And, just off the stage, Erik smiled at me, pleased.

"Your Highness." Gavril bowed as he spoke. "May I say, considering the circumstances under which you've been thrust into this role, you are doing a fantastic job."

"Thank you, sir." I didn't know how genuine that statement was, but maybe him saying it would make other people think it.

"One has to wonder, if you've been working at such a pace, have you made any time for this lot over here?" he asked, nodding his head toward the Elite.

"A little."

"Really? Anything you can share with us?" He wiggled

his eyebrows, and I was reminded again of the ways in which his on-camera personality differed from his off-camera one. Entertainment was his job, and he was great at it.

"Yes, but for fun—I won't be using names."

"Not using names?"

"For instance, one member of the Elite has left us today," I said, though I knew this was a throwaway that'd be unraveled in seconds. "I would like to say of our departed suitor that he left in good spirits and as a friend."

"Ah, I see," Gavril said. "I like this! Give us some more."

"Well, today one of my suitors gave me a gift made from a very precious metal."

"Oh, my!" Gavril surveyed my hands, looking, as everyone would, for rings.

I held them up for the world to see. "No, not gold. It was steel. He gave me a sewing pin. But I promise, it was very special."

Chuckles arose from our audience and from the Elite, and I hoped that this was as charming on camera as it was in my head.

"Please tell me you have at least one more," Gavril pleaded.

"One more," I allowed. "Earlier this week, one of the Elite told me he definitely wasn't in love with me, and I told him I felt the same way."

Gavril was wide-eyed. "Is this the same young man who happened to leave us?"

"No. And that's the crazy part. We're not in love and yet we have no desire to be separated, so there you go." I gave a playful shrug, and smiled as I listened to the sighs and laughter around the room.

"While I'm sure a fair share of our country will be up late tonight trying to guess who you're talking about, it would be nice to have something a bit more solid."

"You might have to talk to the boys about that."

"Then I think we shall do just that. May I go and quiz these handsome young men?"

"By all means," I replied with a smile, happy to back out of the spotlight for one beautiful moment.

"All right, let's start down here. Sir Fox, how are you?"

"Very good, sir. Thank you." He sat up a little straighter and smiled brightly.

"The people understand that the princess has been under a lot of stress and her days are packed full, so the one-on-one time has been limited," Gavril said graciously.

"Yeah, it was impressive to see how hard she was working before, so seeing her take on even more these last few days . . . it's inspiring."

I tipped my head, feeling a little warm inside. Inspiring? That was such a kind thought.

Gavril nodded in agreement. "Considering all that, could you tell us something from your time with the princess that has stood out against all the rest?"

Instantly, a smile came to Fox's face. "I suppose the most significant moment of our relationship would be after the fight, when Burke went home. She came and spoke to me and was so honest about what she hoped for. She listened to me, too. I think that's a side of her that few people have the privilege of seeing. It's not as if she can go door-to-door giving everyone an hour of her time . . . but when she's with you, she's all there. She's really hearing you."

I remembered that night with Fox warmly, but I didn't realize how much it had meant to him. He'd treasured that moment.

Kile raised his hand. "I'd have to agree with that. Everyone knows that Ead—uh, the princess and I really only began our friendship recently. And in that time, I've felt a lot of my worries and aspirations have been heard."

"Like what?" Gavril prodded.

He shrugged. "I mean, it's nothing exciting, but I do have a passion for architecture, and the princess actually sat down and looked at my sketches." He raised a finger as if he suddenly remembered something. "Granted, we'd had some wine, and I'm sure she was very bored, but still."

Everyone chuckled, and I smiled at Kile. He made being on camera look so easy, always coming up with wonderful things to say. It made me feel surer I'd made the right call telling him how I felt.

Carrying the momentum, Gavril bypassed Henri and headed straight to Ean. I hated that Henri was being excluded, but it looked like Gavril had a plan.

"Sir Ean, you are maybe the quietest one of the bunch. Do you have anything to add?"

His expression was as cool as ever. "I am a man of few words," he agreed, "but I will say that the princess is incredibly thoughtful. Though there are only five of us left, none of the eliminations were made flippantly. Just by getting to know these other gentlemen, I can see the effort the princess has put into making the best possible choice for herself and for her people.

"What the cameras couldn't capture was the mood in the Men's Parlor when she had to make her most recent elimination. There wasn't a drop of animosity in the air. She's been so generous with us that it was impossible to be upset. All the other suitors left satisfied."

Gavril nodded. "So how do you think your chances are? You've made it to the top five!"

Ean, as always, was nothing but smooth. "I am at Her Highness's disposal. She is the best woman any of us could possibly attain, and as such has incredible standards. It's not about my assessment of my odds, it's about her preference. For that we will all wait and see."

I'd never heard Ean speak so much at once, but I found myself feeling instantly indebted to him. Though we had an understanding in our relationship, and it was admittedly unromantic, he still saw so much good in me. That, or he was an incredible actor.

"Very interesting. What about you, Sir Hale? As I recall, you had the first date with the princess. How are you feeling right now?"

"I feel lucky," he said warmly. "I've grown up seeing her in parades, and watching her on television, and seeing her face in magazines." He pointed across the room at me. "She's so pretty it's intimidating, and she has this look like maybe she could burn you with her eyes if she felt like it."

Part of that stung, but there was something so terribly honest about it that I couldn't not smile.

"But I got to have dinner with her once and made her laugh so hard she spit her drink out."

"Hale!"

He shrugged. "Someone would find out someday. You might as well share!"

I covered my face with my hands, wondering what Mom and Dad would think of all this.

"My point is, everything we've said about her is true. She's tough, she's a leader, and, yes, I think if she wanted to shoot fire from her eyes, she could do it." The room chuckled. "But she's also a great listener, and is invested, and knows how to laugh. Like, really laugh. I'm not sure everyone will get to see that, so I feel lucky that I did."

The entire segment was such a glorious tribute to my finer qualities that I almost wondered if the boys had been coached. And if they had, then I owed something huge to whoever thought of it.

As the cameras went down, I walked over to Gavril. "Thank you. You were outstanding tonight."

"I have always been on your side, and I always will be." He winked at me and went on his way.

I watched as the audience filtered out, and I stood there a moment feeling proud. I'd gotten through it, almost entirely on my own. The Elite were fantastic, kinder than I could have guessed or hoped. Mom and Dad were going to be so pleased.

"Well done." Kile wrapped an arm around me. "Your first solo *Report* is in the books!"

"I seriously thought tonight might be a disaster, but look!" I said, leaping away and holding out my arms. "I'm still in one piece."

Hale came over and chuckled. "Did you think people would stream in through the doors and tear you to bits?"

"You never know!"

Fox laughed, and Ean stood back, still smiling. I was so grateful. If I'd known how to articulate it, I'd have unabashedly gushed about how great they'd been tonight.

"Dinner?" Fox asked, and the boys all nodded.

I heard Henri saying one word over and over again excitedly, which I assumed meant he was thrilled to be getting food. We all formed a little group and walked to the dining hall together.

CHAPTER 11

I FELT SO CONTENT AS we walked up the stairs and down the hallways, a sense of familiarity and peace surrounding me that I suspected had a lot to do with me feeling so comfortable with my company.

It lasted right up until the moment we walked through the dining-hall doors.

Mom and Dad were still upstairs, and Grandma had retreated to her room. Osten wasn't feeling well this evening, so Kaden was keeping him company, and my twin was still an ocean away from me and then some.

One look at the empty head table and I wanted to go and hide away myself.

"Your Highness?" Erik asked, and I turned to find myself inches away from his concerned eyes. There was something calming about them, a detail I remembered from after the fight in the kitchen. I'd looked into them then and felt like I had seen right through to his soul. Even now, with so many people around, just seeing his crystal-clear blue eyes search mine swept away my sadness. "Are you all right?" he said, and I could tell from his tone that he'd already asked me once and I'd missed it.

"Yes. Could you please go grab those chairs and put them on the other side of the head table? You, too, Ean?" They walked off to follow my request. "Hale, Fox? Can you get the place settings?"

I moved, too, picking up silverware and glasses, and making my way to the head table. Before anyone else could choose a place, I took Dad's chair for myself. Kile was on one side, and Hale was on the other. Fox, Henri, Erik, and Ean sat across from us, and suddenly that long, imposing table felt like an intimate dinner party. Just me and my boys.

The butlers were a little disorganized as they served, unprepared for the impromptu rearrangement but making it to everyone in good time. And, taking a cue from our date, Henri dug in first and the others followed.

"So, I hope you're all ready for tomorrow," I announced. "Erik and Henri are giving us Finnish lessons in the morning."

"Really?" Kile asked excitedly. Erik blushed a little and nodded.

"What's in the lesson plans?" Fox asked.

Erik raised his eyes to the ceiling as if he was still deciding. "Henri and I were talking, and I think we'll bypass the usual first-day things, like the alphabet. What would be most helpful in this situation is basic conversational skills. So telling time and other requests will be at the top of the agenda."

"Neat!" Hale commented. "I've been wanting to learn more. Great idea, Erik."

He shook his head. "It was our future queen's idea. The credit belongs to her."

"Hey," Kile said, getting my attention. "Can we also take a moment to talk about how great you were on the *Report* again? I know you've done announcements and stuff, but managing a whole show on your own is no small feat."

"Also," Fox added, "how awesome is the seating arrangement tonight? For all but one of us, this is the only time we'll ever sit at the head table in the palace. Unforgettable."

"Agreed," Ean added.

And while Henri didn't add much to the conversation, I could tell he was pleased, too. But, of course, it would have been more surprising to see him upset. As Erik caught him up on the conversation, he raised his glass.

"For Eadlyn," he said.

The others put their drinks in the air and chorused his toast. I found myself blinking back happy tears and unable to say a word. Not even *thank you*, though I could tell from the looks in their eyes that it was already understood.

There were plenty of good things for the country to focus on, but with a mass elimination earlier in the week and

Gunner leaving before the *Report*, it looked like I was pushing people away again. At least that's what the papers said. It was as if they didn't hear a single thing Ean had said about how I'd toiled over that decision. An entire live broadcast was brought to rubble by a handful of headlines.

Surprisingly, beneath those stories was Marid's handsome face splashed across the papers next to mine, with commentary on how he'd missed out now that I'd begun my Selection process.

"Give me those," Neena insisted, balling up the papers and smooshing them into the trash can. "It seems they're reporting little news and plenty of gossip these days."

"Undoubtedly," Lady Brice agreed. "Focus less on what people say and more on what you can accomplish."

I nodded my head, knowing she was right. She told me things I felt sure my father would if he was in the room, and though it wasn't always easy, I felt compelled to listen.

"I'm just not sure I can focus on what I'm capable of accomplishing until I get public opinion under control. Anything I propose, even if it is something they might have championed if Mom or Dad had initiated it, will probably be met with opposition. I need to choose a husband," I said decidedly. "I feel confident that will help with public opinion, and let's all hope so, because they don't like me."

"Eadlyn, that's not—"

"It's true. I know it is, Lady Brice. I've experienced it myself. Need I remind you of the parade?"

She crossed her arms. "Okay, fine. You're not exactly

popular. And I can see how finding a partner might sway that. So, is that what we're focusing on today?"

"At least for the next five minutes. I trust my head a little more than my heart, so help me. Talk it out."

Neena shrugged. "Who's up first? Kile? The entire palace is pulling for him. He's so cute and smart and oh, my goodness, if you don't want him, send him my way."

"Don't you have a boyfriend?"

She sighed. "I hate it when you're right."

I laughed. "I'd be lying if I said I didn't feel a connection with him. I even told him as much . . . but I keep pausing on him. I'm not sure why, but I'm not ready to say he's my first choice."

"Okay," Lady Brice replied. "Who else?"

"Hale. He's got a great attitude and has vowed to prove himself to me every day. He's yet to fail. And he's easy to be around. That's one of the reasons I like Fox, too."

"Fox is more attractive than Hale," Neena said. "Not to be shallow, but those things matter in public opinion."

"I understand that, but beauty is subjective. You know how sometimes what makes a person attractive is the way they make you laugh or how it seems like they can read your mind? I want to think about that, too."

Neena smiled. "So you'd pick Hale over Fox then?"

I shook my head. "That's not what I meant exactly. I'm only trying to say that looks aren't everything. We need to focus on other qualities."

"Like?" Lady Brice encouraged.

"Like how Henri is endlessly optimistic. No matter the circumstance, he is a beacon of joy. And I don't doubt his affection for me in the slightest."

Neena rolled her eyes. "That's fine, but he can't speak English. There's no way you two have ever had a conversation that did more than skim the surface."

"That's . . . well, that's true. But he's very sweet and would be good to me. Erik said it was possible for Henri to learn, but it might take a while. And he's been up until midnight studying since he became an Elite. And for my part, I'm on my way to a Finnish lesson right now. We can work on this from both ends, and Erik could stay on for as long as it took for us to adjust."

Lady Brice shook her head. "That's rather unfair to Erik. He has a family, a job. He didn't sign up to possibly be stuck at the palace for the next five years. What if he wants to find a partner of his own?"

I wanted to shoot back that she was wrong . . . but I couldn't. Erik didn't know how long the Selection would last when he agreed to come, but he certainly didn't go into this thinking he'd live at the palace until his charge was fluent in English. And it would be unkind to ask him to do just that.

"He'd stay. I know it," was all I said.

There was a silence after that, like Lady Brice knew I was in the wrong and was debating calling me on it. Instead she sighed.

"Who's left? Ean?" she asked.

"Ean's a little trickier, but trust me, he's important."

Neena squinted. "So then . . . they're all front-runners?"

I sighed. "I guess so. I'm not sure if that means I chose well or chose poorly."

Lady Brice laughed. "You chose well. Really. I may not understand Ean's appeal or how you'd make things work with Henri, but they all have their merits. I think what we need to do at this point is step up their training, really start grooming them for the throne. That will help elevate some of them, I'm sure."

"Grooming? That sounds creepy."

"I don't mean it like that. I'm simply saying—"

Lady Brice's next words were lost because, without any warning, Grandma flung the door open.

"You really need to ask permission first," a guard warned her in a hushed tone.

She kept walking toward me. "Well, my girl, it's time for me to head out."

"So soon?" I asked, embracing her.

"I can never stay too long. Your mother is recovering from a heart attack, and she still has the audacity to order me around. I know she's the queen," she conceded, raising her hands in the air in surrender, "but I'm her mother, and that trumps queen any day."

I laughed. "I'll remember that for down the road."

"You do that," she said, rubbing my cheek. "And if you don't mind, get yourself a husband as soon as you can. I'm not getting any younger, and I'd like to see at least one great-grandchild before I'm dead." She stared at my stomach and shook her finger. "Don't let me down."

"Ooooookay, Grandma. We have to get back to work here, so you head on home and make sure to call when you get there."

"Will do, honey. Will do."

I stood in silence, basking in the insanity that was my grandmother.

Neena leaned over. "Now, which of your top five do you think would be the most eager baby maker? Should we put that on a checklist?"

Even my most violent glare did nothing to diminish her giddiness. "Don't forget, I can call in a firing squad at any moment if I like."

"You can call that firing squad whenever you want, but I've got Grandma on my side, so I've got nothing to worry about."

I slumped, letting the silliness of it all settle in. "Sadly, Neena, I think you're right."

"Don't feel too bad. She means well at the heart of it all."

"I'll try and remember that. So are we okay for now? I need to go learn some Finnish."

"Sorry, sorry, sorry!" I said, bursting into the library. The boys cheered at my entrance, and I scurried over to an open seat at a table with Henri, Hale, and Ean. "Duty called."

Erik chuckled, placing a small packet of papers in front of me. "You're excused. Don't worry. We haven't gotten too far. Look over the first page, and Henri will help you with pronunciations while I check how everyone else is doing. Then we'll move on."

"Okay." I picked up the paper—a copy made of Erik's handwritten notes with hand-drawn pictures in the margin—and smiled. First task of the day was learning to count to twelve, so we could tell time. Staring at this simple lesson made me instantly embarrassed. All I could think of was that it seemed there weren't enough vowels in the words, and the ones that bothered to show up were all in the wrong places. "All right," I said, looking at the first word: *yksi.*

"*Yucksey?*"

Henri giggled and shook his head. "Is said *yoo-ksi.*"

"*Yooksi?*"

"Yes! Go, go," he encouraged, and though I couldn't be anything close to perfect, it was still nice having my own personal cheerleader. "Is said *kahk-si.*"

"*Kahk-si . . . kaksi.*"

"Good, good. Now, is *kolme.*"

"*Coolmay,*" I tried.

"Ehhh," he said, still trying to be positive. "*Kohl-may.*"

I tried again, but I could see I was getting it wrong. I was being foiled by the number three. Ever the gentleman, he leaned in, preparing to take as much time as I needed.

"Is said *oh. Kohl-may.*"

"*Ooh. Ooh,*" I tried.

He lifted his hand and gently put his fingers on my cheeks, trying to change the shape of my mouth, and it tickled. I broke into a smile, unable to even make the sound he was going for in the first place. But he held my face all the same. After a moment, the humor left his eyes, and I recognized the look in them. I'd seen it before, in the kitchen, when he'd turned his shirt into an apron for me.

It was such a captivating stare, I completely forgot there were other people in the room.

Until Erik dropped a book on the other desk. "Excellent," he said, and I pulled away from Henri as quickly as I could, praying that no one had noticed what had nearly just happened.

"It looks like you're all doing well with the numbers, so we're going to start using them in sentences. If you'll look up at the board here, I've got a written example; but as I'm sure you've already guessed, the pronunciation is a bit tricky."

The boys laughed, seeming to have struggled with the numbers as much as I had . . . and also seeming to have been too engrossed to have noted my almost kiss. I focused my gaze on the board, trying to take in the phonetics of the words in front of me instead of focusing on how close Henri was sitting.

CHAPTER 12

THE FIRST FREE MOMENT I had that day was lunch, and I knew I needed to use the time to focus on damage control. While everyone headed off to the dining room after our Finnish lesson, I went back to my office and pulled Marid's card from my desk drawer. It was clearly made from expensive paper. I wondered what his family was doing now to afford that. They must have done well for themselves, wherever their path had taken them.

I dialed the number, kind of hoping he wouldn't pick up.

"Hello?"

"Yes, um, Marid?"

"Eadlyn, is that you?"

"Yes." I fidgeted, straightening out my clothes, even though he couldn't see me. "Is this an okay time?"

"Absolutely. How can I help you, Your Highness?"

"I just wanted to say, I saw some speculation about our relationship in the press the other day."

"Oh, yeah. I'm sorry about that. You know how they can take a thing out of context."

"I do," I nearly exclaimed. "And really, I wanted to apologize to you. I know what an upheaval it can be when someone's life is caught up in mine, and I'm sorry you've been going through that."

"Eh, let 'em talk," he replied with a laugh. "Really, no apology necessary. But while I've got you, I wanted to run an idea past you."

"Sure."

"I know you've been worried about the post-caste violence, and I thought it might be good for you to have something like a town hall session."

"What do you mean?"

"You could choose a handful of people from various backgrounds to come to the palace and sit down with you personally. It would be a unique opportunity to hear from your people, and if you invited the press, it might also be a rather spectacular opportunity to show how well the palace listens to its people."

I was stunned. "Actually, that's a wonderful idea."

"If you want, I can take care of most of the arrangements for you. I have a few links with some families that used to be Eights, as well as some that have had a hard time letting go of their Two status. Maybe we could plan on inviting a dozen or so people, so you wouldn't be overwhelmed?"

"Marid, that sounds perfect. I'm going to have my lady-in-waiting call you. Her name is Neena Hallensway, and she's as organized as you seem to be. She knows my schedule and would be the best person to talk to about a time and date."

"Excellent. I'll wait to hear from her."

There was a long silence, and I wasn't quite sure how to break away.

"Thank you," I tried. "Now more than ever, I really need to prove how much I care about my people. I want them to know that, in a few years, I'll be as able to lead them as my father."

"How anyone could doubt that is a mystery to me."

I smiled, thrilled to have added another ally to my arsenal. "Sorry to rush off, but I must be going."

"Not at all. We'll talk again soon."

"Of course. Good-bye."

"Good-bye."

I hung up the phone and sighed in relief. That wasn't as awkward as I'd been fearing it would be. Marid's words rang in my ears. *Let 'em talk.* I knew they always would. Hopefully soon, they'd have something positive to say.

CHAPTER 13

"WAIT, WHICH WAY DO THESE guys move again?" Hale asked before reaching over and picking up two petits fours and setting them on his plate.

"Bishops move diagonally. I wouldn't do that if I was you, but it's your funeral."

He laughed. "Okay. What about the little castle ones?"

"Straight lines, either side to side or back and forth."

He moved his rook, taking another one of my pawns. "Honestly, I never would have pegged you for a chess girl."

"I'm not really. Ahren used to be obsessed, and he forced me to play with him every single day for months. But then he got serious about Camille, and all his chess time turned into letter-writing time."

I moved my bishop and took his knight.

"Ugh, I didn't even see that," he lamented between bites.

"I've been wanting to ask you about Ahren, but I wasn't sure if you were up for it."

I shrugged, prepared to dismiss the invitation, but instead I reminded myself that if I was going to have a shot at happiness at all, I had to let someone past my walls. Sighing, I told the truth.

"I miss him. It's like I grew up with a built-in best friend, and now he's gone. I have other people I'm close to, like my lady-in-waiting, Neena. I don't think I realized how much I was relying on her until Ahren was gone and I could see it. But it makes me afraid. What if I get to the point I did with Ahren, where she's the person I go to with everything, and then something happens and she leaves?"

Hale nodded as he listened, and I could see he was trying to suppress a smile.

"This isn't funny!" I complained, chucking one of his lost pawns at him.

He laughed out loud, dodging the throw. "No, I'm not smiling because of that. It's just . . . the last time we talked like this you ran. You're not wearing sneakers under that gown, are you?"

"Not at all. They wouldn't go together," I teased. "No, really, I should have trusted you then, and I do trust you now. Sorry if I'm slow. Opening up to people is not a skill of mine."

"No rush. I'm a pretty patient person."

I couldn't take the eye contact anymore, so I focused on

the board, watching his hands hover above the grid.

"As for how you feel about Neena," Hale went on, "even if she did have to leave, that wouldn't make her less of a friend any more than it makes Ahren less of your brother. You might have to work harder to keep in touch, but if you love them as much as you say, it'll be worth it."

"I know that's true," I admitted. "It's already pretty difficult for me to make friends, seeing as I don't get out much. So I kind of need to keep the ones I have."

Hale chuckled, and I missed what he did on the board. "Well, I just want to go on record and say that even if you don't choose me, you have my friendship for life, and I'll be on a plane to Angeles in a heartbeat if you ever need me."

I smiled. "Something every day."

He nodded. "Every day."

"I really needed to hear that. Thank you." I sat up taller and began to plan my next move. "What about you? Who's your best friend?"

"Actually, I was interrogated over this a few weeks ago, just after Burke left. My best friend is a girl, and they thought I was writing to 'my girlfriend back home.' Let me tell you, it was humiliating to ask her to get on the phone with a guard and explain that we'd never, *ever* been romantically involved."

I bit my lip, glad he could see the humor in it. "I'm really sorry."

"It's fine. Carrie got a kick out of it, actually."

"Well, I'm happy she took it in stride." I cleared my throat.

"But now I have to ask, have you really never had a crush on her?"

"No!" He almost shuddered. "Carrie's like a sister to me. The thought of kissing her just feels wrong."

I put my hands up in front of me, startled by how offended he was. "Okay. I don't have to worry about Carrie. Got it."

"Sorry." The disgust in his face shifted to a shy smile. "It's just that I've been asked that a million times. Other friends, our parents . . . it's like everyone has always wanted us to be together, and I don't feel anything like that for her."

"I get that. Sometimes it seems like everyone wants me to pick Kile just because we grew up together. Like that alone is enough to guarantee you'll fall in love."

"Well, the difference there is that you actually have feelings for Kile. Anyone watching could tell." He fiddled with a discarded pawn.

I looked at my lap. "I shouldn't have brought that up. I'm sorry."

"No, it's okay. I think the only way to stay sane through all this is to remember that you're the one leading this, and you're the one who decides where we stand. The only thing any of us can do is be ourselves."

"Where do you think you stand exactly?"

He gave me a small smile. "I don't know. Somewhere in the middle?"

I shook my head. "You're doing better than that."

"Yeah?"

"Yeah."

His smile faded a little. "That's kind of amazing, but also scary. There's a lot of responsibility that comes with winning this."

I nodded. "Tons."

"I guess I never really stopped to think about that. But with you really being in charge these days, it's a little . . . overwhelming."

I stared at him, feeling certain I had to be misunderstanding something. "You're not trying to back out, are you?"

"No," he said, continuing to roll the pawn in his hand. "I'm just coming face-to-face with how big this is. I'm sure your mom had moments like this, too."

He was uncharacteristically sharp, and this seemed to run deeper than his frustration about Carrie. As I continued, trying to keep my tone even, he avoided my eyes.

"Did I miss something? You've always been so enthusiastic, to the point that I've wondered about your sanity. What's with the sudden cold feet?"

"I didn't say I was having cold feet," he countered. "I was simply voicing a concern. You're constantly voicing your concerns. How is this any different?"

There was plenty of truth to that, but I had clearly hit a nerve. And after how hard I'd worked to be open with Hale, I didn't understand why he would clam up on me. While I didn't think he was the type to test me simply for the sake of it, I wondered if maybe he was trying to gauge my patience.

I clenched and unclenched my hands underneath the table, reminding myself that I trusted Hale.

"Perhaps it's better if we change the subject," I suggested.

"Agreed."

But the only thing that followed was silence.

CHAPTER 14

THE PARLOR WAS PREPARED FOR our coming guests. Two
rows of chairs were set up stadium style, reminding me of
how the Selected used to sit for the *Report*. We had food and
drinks around the room, a security checkpoint by the door,
and cameras circulating.

Behind the production staff, the Elite sat against the wall,
and they all seemed to be excited to find a part of my job
they could observe. I was happy to see that Kile and Erik
(though surely his actions were more for Henri's benefit) had
both brought notepads. They'd come to work.

"You look lovely," Marid assured me, probably noting
that I was pulling at my collar.

"I was trying to look businesslike without making things
too formal."

"And you succeeded. You just need to calm down. They're

not here to attack you; they're here to talk to you. The only thing you have to do is listen."

I nodded. "Listen. I can do that." I took a deep breath. We'd never done anything like this before, and I was equal parts giddy and horrified. "How did you find these people? Friends of yours?"

"Not exactly. A few have called in to radio shows I've done before, and others were suggested by acquaintances. It's a good mix of social and economic statuses, which should create some well-rounded discussion."

I took this in. That's all this was: a discussion. I would see the faces of people who actually lived in our country, hear their voices. It wasn't a massive crowd; it was a handful.

"We're going to make it through this, all right?" he said reassuringly.

"All right." And I reminded myself that this was a good thing as our guests began trickling into the room.

I walked over to shake hands with a woman who looked like she'd taken more time on her hair than I had and her husband who, while handsome, could have knocked some-one out with the amount of cologne he'd put on.

"Your Highness," the woman greeted, dropping into a curtsy. "My name is Sharron Spinner, and this is my hus-band, Don." He bowed. "We're so pleased to be here. It's so nice the palace is taking time to hear from its people."

I nodded. "It's long overdue. Please, help yourself to some refreshments and make yourself comfortable. The producers might stop to interview you as people settle in, but you're under no obligation to speak to them if you don't want to."

Sharron touched the corners of her lips, making sure her makeup was as pristine as possible. "No, we don't mind at all. Come on, honey."

I could barely contain my eye roll. The Spinners seemed a little too eager to be on camera.

Behind the Spinners were the Barnses and the Palters. There was a girl on her own, Bree Marksman, and two younger men, Joel and Blake, who had met in the foyer and were already talking like friends. Finally a younger couple who introduced themselves as the Shells walked in. They looked like they had done their best to scrape together some nice clothes for the occasion and had come up short.

"Brenton and Ally, you said?" I waved a hand, inviting them to walk beside me.

"Yes, Your Highness. Thank you so much for having us." Brenton smiled, looking grateful and bashful at once. "Does this mean that we're going to be able to move now?"

I stopped, turning to face them. Ally swallowed, clearly trying not to get her hopes up.

"Move?"

"Yeah. Down in Zuni we've been trying to move out of our neighborhood for a while."

"It's not very safe," Ally added quietly.

"We've been thinking about starting a family. But they keep changing the prices of the apartments."

"We had friends who moved, and they didn't have any problems," Ally insisted.

"But when we tried to get into the same area, the rent was double what it was for Nic and Ellen."

"The owners said our friends must have misquoted the rate, but . . . well, I don't want to accuse anyone of anything, but Nic was born a Three, and we both would be Fives.

"We just want to live somewhere safer," Brenton added with a shrug. "Even if you can't fix it, we thought meeting with the princess might help things."

"Your Highness," the producer said. "I'm sorry to interrupt, but we're starting." She showed the Shells to their seats, and I sat across from everyone, unsure of how to begin.

I laughed, trying to break the tension. "Since we've never done this before, we don't really have an outline to follow. Does anyone have any questions?"

One of the young men—Blake, I remembered—raised his hand, and I watched as cameras changed angles to focus on his face.

"Yes, Blake?"

"When will the king be back?"

And, just like that, I became insignificant. "I'm not sure. It depends on when my mother is fully recovered."

"But he will be back, right?"

I forced myself to smile. "If, for some reason, he didn't return, the state would continue as usual. I have always been next in line to rule, and I have the same ideals as my father. He wanted so badly to see the castes brought to an end, and now that they're gone, I would seek to further erase the lines they've left in their wake."

I peeked over at Marid, who gave me a quick thumbs-up.

"But that's the thing," Andrew Barns began. "The palace has done nothing to help those of us whose parents were Fives and Sixes or lower."

"I think we've been at a loss as to what would be most effective. That's part of why you're here today. We want to hear from you." I crossed my hands on my lap, hoping I looked put together.

"Do monarchs ever really hear their people?" Bree asked. "Have you considered handing the government over to the public? Don't you think there's a chance we might do a better job than you?"

"Well—"

Sharron cut me off, turning to Bree. "Sweetie, you can barely dress yourself. How do you think you could possibly run a country?"

"Give me a vote!" Bree demanded. "That alone would change plenty."

Mr. Palter—Jamal—leaned forward. "You're too young," he said, also ganging up on Bree. "I want to see change myself. I've lived through the castes. I was a Three, and I lost a lot since then. You kids don't know enough about where we've been to even contribute to the conversation."

The other single boy stood up, enraged. "Just because I'm young doesn't mean I don't pay attention or that I don't know people who've struggled. I want this country to be better for everyone, not just me."

We were less than five minutes in, and the entire

conversation had turned into a barking contest. It didn't even seem to matter that I was there. Plenty of people mentioned me, of course, but no one actually spoke to me.

I supposed trying to get a glimpse at a wide range of lifestyles meant we were going to have conflict, but I wished Marid had vetted these people better. Then again, maybe he had, and we still ended up with people who didn't care if I was present or not. I'd spent so much time worrying that they'd hate me that I hadn't paused to consider the possibility that I was simply irrelevant in their eyes.

"If we could maybe raise our hands," I suggested, trying to regain control. "I can't hear your thoughts if you're all speaking at once."

"I demand a vote!" Bree yelled, and the others fell silent. She glared at me. "You people have no idea what our lives are actually like. Look at this room." She gestured to the expertly coordinated paint and tapestries, the porcelain dishes and sparkling glasses. "How can we trust your judgment when you are this disconnected from your people? You rule over our lives with no understanding of what it means to live the way we do."

"She has a point," said Suzette Palter. "You've never spent a day in the dirt or on the run. It's easy to make decisions about other people's lives when you don't have to live them."

I sat there, staring at these strangers. I was responsible for them. But how could I be? How could one person make sure each and every soul had every chance they could, everything they needed? It wasn't possible. And yet, stepping down didn't seem like the solution either.

"I'm sorry, I have to stop this," Marid said, coming out of the shadows. "The princess is too gracious to remind you of exactly who she is, but as her very dear friend, I cannot allow you to speak to her this way."

He reminded me of some of my tutors, the way they stood over me and made me feel embarrassed even when I wasn't sure there was a reason I should be.

"Princess Eadlyn may not be your sovereign today, but she is destined for the throne. She has earned it through a long line of tradition and sacrifice. You forget that while you have choice over your profession, location, your very future, hers has been assigned to her at birth. And she has willingly accepted the weight of it for your sake.

"Shouting at her over her youth is unfair, as we all know her father had little more experience when he ascended. Princess Eadlyn has studied tirelessly at his side for years and has already said she plans to carry out his ambitions. Tell her how to do that."

Bree cocked her head. "I already did."

"If you're suggesting we suddenly become a democracy, that would cause more havoc in your life than you can imagine," Marid insisted.

"But if you want a vote," I began, "perhaps we can talk about how to implement that locally. It's much more possible for the leaders closest to you, the ones who actually see your area day to day, to provide what's needed most for you."

Bree didn't smile, but she did relax her tight shoulders. "That would be a start."

"Okay then." I saw Neena ferociously taking notes. "Brenton, you mentioned something about housing when you came in. Can you tell me more about that?"

After fifteen minutes the group came to the decision that housing should never be denied to anyone based on their profession or former caste, and that all prices should be made public so they couldn't be marked up to restrict certain people from applying.

"I don't want to sound snobby," Sharron said, "but some of us live in areas where we would prefer . . . certain people not to come."

"You failed," one of the boys said. "That sounds completely snobby."

I sighed, thinking. "First of all, I assume that if you live in a wealthy neighborhood, it would take a considerable amount of money to move there in the first place. And second of all, you're assuming that people with little means would make for horrible neighbors.

"What you said about me, Suzette, was right." She perked up at the sound of her name and smiled over being correct without knowing what it was yet. "I've never lived outside the palace. But thanks to the Selection, young men from many different backgrounds have come into my life, and they've taught me so much. Some of them were working through school or supporting their families or trying just to master English so they can have more opportunities. They might have gone through their lives with much less than I have, but they've enriched my life in ways I can't begin to express. Sharron?" I asked. "Isn't that worth something?"

She didn't answer.

"At the end of the day, I can't force any of you to treat people the way you should. But it should be on your conscience that whatever laws I pass won't do much unless each of you takes it upon yourself to show kindness to your fellow citizens."

I saw Marid smile and knew that while I may not have gotten it perfect, I'd taken a big step. It felt like a victory.

When the town hall meeting was over, I felt ready to collapse from the tension. Nearly two hours of talking felt like a week's worth of work. Thank goodness the Elite seemed to understand how drained I was and left with little more than polite bows. There'd be plenty of time to discuss this with them later. For now I just wanted to flop onto a couch.

I groaned at Marid. "I get the feeling they'll want us to do this again, but I refuse until I have fully recovered from today. Which may take years."

He laughed. "You did great. They're the ones who made it difficult. But since this was a first, no one knew how to behave. If you do this again, it will be much better on all sides."

"I hope so." I rubbed my hands together. "I keep thinking about Bree, how passionate she was."

"Passionate." He rolled his eyes. "That's one word for it."

"I'm serious. This mattered so much to her," I lamented,

thinking of how she looked close to tears a few times. "I've studied political science my whole life. I know about republics and constitutional monarchies and democracies. I wonder if maybe she's right. Maybe we should—"

"Let me stop you right there. Have you already forgotten how deranged she looked when she saw she wasn't going to get her way? Do you really want the country's choices made by someone like her?"

"She's one voice out of millions."

"Exactly. And I have studied politics just as long as you and through a much more varied lens. Trust me, it is far better to keep the control right here." He held my hands in his, smiling so surely that I dismissed my thoughts. "And you are very capable. Don't let a tiny group of people with no idea of how to reasonably voice their opinions undermine your confidence."

I nodded. "I was a bit shaken, that's all."

"Of course you were. That was a tough crowd. But you could wash it all away with a bottle of wine. I know you have excellent stores here."

"We do," I replied with a grin.

"Come on, then. Let's celebrate. You just did a wonderful thing for your people. You've more than earned a glass."

CHAPTER 15

"WELL, IT WASN'T GREAT," I admitted, "but it could have been much worse."

"Tell your daughter to give herself more credit," Marid insisted.

Mom and Dad smiled, and I was glad we'd run into them in the hallway. Dad's voice, above all the others, would help me sort out exactly what I'd just said and done.

"We try, Marid, I assure you." Dad took a sip of his wine before setting it down, pushing it far away, and pouring himself a cup of tea, just like Mom.

The doctor said an occasional drink was fine, but she clearly wasn't interested in risking it, and I wasn't surprised Dad would follow her lead.

"How's your mother?" Mom asked. The set of her lips made me feel like she'd been dying to ask the question.

Marid grinned. "She never slows down. She's sad, of course, that she can't do bigger things, but she works diligently to take care of those near us in Columbia. Even a small bit of good is better than none."

"Agreed," Mom replied. "Would you please tell her I think of her often?"

She flicked her eyes toward Dad, who remained unreadable, but Marid seemed pleased. "I will. And I can assure you, she feels the same."

The conversation paused, and everyone focused on their drinks for a moment. Finally, Dad saved us from the silence.

"So it sounds like that one couple was borderline vicious. The wife, what was her name?"

"Sharron," Marid and I chorused back.

Dad shook his head. "She came in with an agenda."

"They all did," I said. "But wasn't that the point? Everyone probably has a specific idea of how to improve their day-to-day life. The hard part wasn't that they had those thoughts—it was how they were trying to get them across."

Mom nodded. "There has to be a way to do something like this without all the arguing. It slows everything down."

"In some ways, but in others it adds to the discussion," Marid claimed. "Once they were reminded of who they were speaking with, the conversation became much clearer."

"I definitely think there was more positive than negative today," I added.

Dad was looking down at the table.

"Dad? Don't you think so?"

He looked up at me, smiling. "Yes, dear. I do." He sighed, straightening his posture. "And I owe you thanks, Marid. A move like this is certainly progress, not just for the palace, but for the country—and it was a very good idea."

"I will pass along your thanks to my father. He put the idea in my head years ago."

Dad grimaced. "Then I also owe you an apology." He tapped his finger on the table, collecting his thoughts. "Please tell your parents they needn't stay away. Just because we disagreed on methods doesn't mean—"

Marid raised his hand. "Say no more, Your Majesty. My father has said on more than one occasion that he stepped over the line. I will urge him to call. Soon."

Dad smiled. "I'd like that."

"Me, too," Mom added.

"And you are welcome to visit as often as you like," I added. "Especially if you have any more thoughts on how to reach our people."

Marid's face was triumphant. "Oh, I have plenty."

The following morning I was almost first to the office, beating everyone except for General Leger, who was rooting around rather forcefully in my father's desk drawers.

"General?" I asked, announcing myself.

He bowed curtly and went back to his search. "Sorry. Your father has broken his glasses, and he said there was another pair in his desk. I'm having no luck at all."

His voice was gruff, and he shoved the drawer closed

before turning around to scan the shelf behind him.

"General Leger?"

"He said they would be here. Are they right in front of me and I'm missing them?"

"Sir?"

"One thing, that's all I had to do. I can't even find a pair of glasses."

"General?"

"Yes?" he replied without looking at me.

"Are you all right?"

"Of course." He searched and searched, not pausing until I laid a gentle hand on his shoulder.

"You wouldn't lie to my father. Please don't lie to me."

He finally looked up from his task, bewilderment in his eyes. "When did you get so tall?" he asked. "And so eloquent? I feel like it was just yesterday that your mother was rushing into the room to get us to come watch your first steps." He smiled a little. "I don't know if you know, but Ahren nearly beat you to the punch. But even back then, you weren't going to let anyone show you up."

"You still haven't answered my question. Are you okay?"

He nodded. "I will be. I've never been good at accepting defeat, even when it was the best thing. Lucy's actually taking this better than I am, though not by much." He squinted. "I assume you know what I'm talking about."

I sighed. "I do. But only barely. I'm embarrassed to admit I've been so focused on myself I didn't realize how much you'd struggled. I wish I'd been more sensitive about all this."

"Don't blame yourself. We don't live in the palace, and not having a family isn't something we willingly chat about. Besides, there's nothing anyone can do about it."

"Nothing?"

"Like I said, we're accepting defeat. In the beginning we thought we had so much time, and when we tried to get help, it just kept falling through. Lucy can't take it anymore." He paused, swallowing before he gave me a weak smile. "I hope I've done right by you. As an official, as a friend. You're the closest I'll ever have to a daughter, so that matters to me."

I found myself near tears, thinking of how I'd called him a backup parent not that long ago. "You have. Of course you have. And not just by me but by every other child in this palace you helped raise."

He squinted.

"Mr. Woodwork had a broken leg when Kile was ready to learn to ride a bike. I remember you running behind him on the gravel in front of the palace until he finally figured out how to balance."

General Leger nodded, the ghost of a grin on his face. "That's true. I did that."

"And Mom and Dad were in New Asia when Kaden lost his first tooth, right? Miss Lucy was the one who helped him get it out. And she taught Josie how to put on eyeliner. Don't you remember how she bragged about it for weeks?"

"What I remember is Marlee telling her to wipe it off," he said, his spirits rising.

"And you taught Ahren and Kaden how to handle a saber.

Kaden recently suggested a duel, and the first thing I thought of was how he would have won hands down thanks to you."

General Leger watched me. "I treasure those memories. I do. I'd defend all of you to my last breath. Even if I wasn't essentially paid to."

I giggled. "I know. Which is why there's no one else I'd trust with my life." I reached out for his hand. "Please take the day off. No one's going to invade today, and if they do, I'll call you," I added quickly when I could see he was going to protest. "Go spend time with Miss Lucy. Remind her of every good thing you've been to each other, and remind her of everything you've been to us. I know it's not a reasonable substitute, but do it all the same."

"I haven't found the glasses yet."

"I'm sure he's left them in the parlor. I'll take care of it. You go."

He gripped my hand one last time before letting it go and dropping into a bow. "Yes, Your Highness."

I watched him leave, leaning against the desk as I considered the general and Miss Lucy and their life together. They'd faced so much sadness, so much disappointment, and yet he still showed up every day, ready to serve. So did Miss Lucy. It was a strange thing to measure them beside my parents, whose lives had seemed to fall into place perfectly.

I was surrounded by examples of how love, real love, could make you less bothered by your circumstances, whether it was facing the greatest disappointment of your life or shouldering the weight of a country. And suddenly, for the life of me, I couldn't remember why I'd been so afraid of it.

I mentally thumbed through my list of suitors. Kile's sweetness, Fox's enthusiasm, Henri's joy . . . these were all things that drew me in. But, beyond that, was there something beautiful and lasting?

I still didn't know. But finding out no longer looked so frightening.

I shook the thought away for the moment and headed into the parlor. Sure enough, Dad's glasses were sitting, unfolded and upside down, on a pile of books. I carried them toward his room, still wondering about the future. In an effort to keep from waking Mom, in case she was sleeping, I knocked on the door to his personal study.

"Yes?" he called.

I walked in to find Dad at his desk, squinting at some papers.

"I found these," I said, holding up his glasses and wiggling them between my fingers.

"Ah! You're a lifesaver. Where's Aspen?" he asked, happily taking the glasses and popping them on his face.

"I told him to take the day off. He seemed a little down."

Dad's head snapped up. "Was he? I didn't notice."

"Yes. He, and I think maybe Miss Lucy, are having a bad day."

At the mention of her name, he seemed to understand.

"Well, now I feel awful for not saying something." He leaned back in his chair and rubbed at his temple.

"Have you been sleeping much?" I asked, fiddling with a paperweight.

He smiled. "I'm trying, honey, really. But if your mom makes so much as a peep, I'm instantly awake, and I end up watching her for an hour before I'm calm enough to sleep again. That heart attack sneaked up on us. If anything, I'd have expected for something to happen to me."

I nodded. So many times recently I'd found myself watching him, wondering if he was okay. But Mom? She blindsided us all.

"Your mom keeps talking about going on the *Report* tomorrow like it's some sign of things getting back to normal. As if, since she can do that, I should go back to work. And I know the second I go back to work, she will, too. I'm not saying I want her to sit around and twiddle her thumbs, but the thought of her going back to being the queen, all day, every day . . . I don't know how to take it."

He rubbed his eyes and gave me a humorless smile. "And the truth is, it's been nice to pause, take a breath. I don't think I realized how hard I'd been running until I had to stop." He looked up at me. "I can't remember the last time I had ten undisturbed hours with my wife. She's got these pretty little laugh lines by her eyes."

I smiled. "Well, you tell a lot of horrible jokes, Dad."

He nodded. "What can I say? I'm a man of many talents. But that's almost as hard to take: when she goes back to being queen, I need to go back to being king. And I don't know when I'll get another week like this, where it's just her and me."

"So, what if she didn't?"

He squinted. "What do you mean?"

"Well . . ." It had been circulating in my head since the town hall meeting yesterday. I'd probably never be able to help all my people, but I could reach a few. That thought thrilled me more than I imagined possible. And, at the very least, I could help my parents, which recently started feeling like a monumental accomplishment. Still, as the words came out, I knew they were pure insanity. "What if she wasn't queen anymore? What if I was?"

Dad stilled, staring at me in disbelief.

"I don't mean it as an insult," I stammered. "I know you're fully able to lead . . . but you're right. Mom's going to want to go back to the complete role of being a queen. If I was queen, she'd have to do something else."

His eyes widened as if he hadn't considered this option.

"And if she wasn't queen and you weren't king, and this time it happened to be while she wasn't recovering from a heart attack, maybe you could do more than sit around. Maybe you could travel or something."

He blinked, astonished at the possibility.

"We could do it this week even. I can have a coronation dress made, Lady Brice and Neena can organize everything, and you know General Leger would make sure the entire event was safe. You wouldn't have to worry about a thing."

He swallowed, looking away. "Please, Dad, I don't mean it as an insult. I—"

He held up a hand, and I silenced myself, stunned to see tears in his eyes when he turned back to me. "I'm not insulted," he answered gruffly before clearing his throat. "I'm just so proud of you."

I smiled. "So . . . you'll let me ascend?"

"You'll have a difficult time," he said seriously. "The people are restless."

"I know. I'm not scared. Well, not *that* scared."

We shared a laugh. "You'll be wonderful."

I shrugged. "I'm no you. And I'm definitely no Mom. But I can do this. I have help, and I'll still have the both of you. And between all of us, I'll probably come out looking like a decent queen."

He shook his head. "You are more than decent, Eadlyn. Maybe I haven't told you enough, but you're an extraordinary young woman. Bright and funny and capable. What a privilege it will be to be your subject." His words were so genuine that I found myself blinking back tears.

I didn't realize how much his opinion of my actions mattered until that moment. I should have, though, considering how many steps I'd taken at his suggestion. It meant the world that he approved of ones I was taking on my own.

He took a deep breath. "Okay, then." Standing, he walked around the table and slid his signet ring off his ring finger and onto the middle finger of my hand. His eyes, the clearest I'd seen them in days, stared deeply into mine. "That looks rather nice on you."

I tilted my head. "Nearly everything does."

CHAPTER 16

WHEN MOM WALKED INTO THE studio on Friday evening, the entire room broke out in applause. She lifted her hand in a wave, acknowledging the support as Dad walked so close beside her you couldn't see a speck of light between them. She had a tiny limp from where the doctors had removed the vein from her leg, but she was so graceful, you really had to look to see it. She'd chosen a dress with a high neckline, and I could tell by the way she kept touching it that she was anxious about her scar.

"You look wonderful," I said, stepping in stride with her and Dad, trying to distract her.

"Thank you. So do you."

"How are you feeling, Dad?" I leaned around her, trying to gauge his emotions.

He tilted his head from side to side. "Part relieved, part

nervous. Not about you—you'll do fine. I'm just concerned about the reaction."

I noted that he looked a bit more rested, and I could tell that seeing Mom all dressed up lifted his spirits.

"Me, too. But we knew this day would come sooner or later. I'd rather do it now and help when it's most useful."

Mom let out a wistful sigh. "Finally out of the spotlight and into the background," she said. "I've missed it there."

"People will still watch, my dear," Dad said. "Just try to keep your chin up tonight, and I'll be right beside you if you need me."

"So, same as always?"

He smiled. "Same as always."

"Look, I don't plan to kick you out or anything, but if you insist on being mushy all the time, I'll have you in a cottage faster than you can say *P-D-A*."

Mom kissed my head. "Good luck tonight."

They made their way to the chairs while I walked across to the boys.

"Your Highness." Ean sank into a bow, his smile brighter than usual.

"Hello, sir."

"How are you tonight?"

"Good, I think. It's going to be a very exciting show."

He leaned in. "I'm always up for a little excitement," he whispered.

Ean smelled of aftershave and tobacco, and as there had been since the moment we'd met, something slightly hypnotic filled the air around him.

"I've been very busy lately, but I've been wondering if you and I should have a date soon."

He shrugged. "Only if you want one. As I said, I have no intention of demanding anything from you."

"So you're quite comfortable?"

"I am," he answered with a smile. "And as always, I'm here for you in whatever capacity you need me."

He bowed and walked away, sitting down next to Hale, who whispered something to Ean as he approached. I watched Ean shake his head in reply. Hale looked unsettled, and I realized we hadn't spoken since our disaster of a date. I wasn't sure if I was ready to cross that bridge yet.

I walked over to my small group of suitors all the same.

"It's so great to see the queen back," Fox said.

I beamed. "It is. She'll be giving a small update about her condition, there will be the normal notes from the advisers, then my father will be making a big announcement. You're off the hook for tonight."

"Thank goodness." Kile slumped back in his seat, grinning.

I chuckled. "I know the feeling. So just sit there and look handsome."

"Done," Ean joked, a thing I hadn't thought him capable of doing. Hale laughed and Henri smiled, though his expression showed me that he didn't understand what had happened.

I started walking away, shaking my head as I went, when

I was caught by the light brush of fingers across my wrist.

"I'm sorry, Your Highness," Erik said. "I was wondering if I should sit with the audience since there won't be any questions tonight."

His blue eyes caught the bright lights of the studio, brilliant and clear.

"Are you afraid I'll drag you into the middle of the set if you don't hide?"

He chuckled. "More than you know."

"Don't worry. You're safe. But Henri will need to understand my father's announcement, so stay close."

He nodded. "I will. Are you all right? You look a little on edge."

"I am. Very much," I confessed.

"Anything I can do for you?"

I placed a hand on his shoulder. "Cross your fingers. It's going to be an interesting night."

I took my seat next to Mom, looking out at the small crowd. Josie's clothing choice baffled me once again. She was covered in so many sequins, one might have thought she was going to be on camera tonight. Maybe that was her plan, to be prepared in case it ever happened.

General Leger usually stood, but tonight he was seated next to Miss Lucy, and she leaned into him. He turned his head slightly to give her the gentlest kiss along her hairline. Neither of them looked at each other or spoke, but I could tell there was some wordless communication happening, and they both seemed lost in the moment.

I could have watched them for hours, but I got distracted. Kaden waved wildly, holding two thumbs up, and I smirked, giving him a small wave in reply.

"If he's that excited about what's coming, imagine how excited Ahren will be when he hears." Mom tugged at her necklace again, arranging all her protective layers.

"Yeah," I answered lamely, thinking that if he couldn't even call me to tell me how he was, he might not be excited at all.

The cameras rolled, and the show began.

Mom opened the *Report* with assurances that she was on the mend. "I'm doing wonderfully, thanks to the work of our excellent doctors and the care of my family," she promised. I knew that this was the only news that would matter to the audience until our big announcement. I could barely pay attention to the updates on funding and international relations myself; I doubted the rest of the country could.

Finally Dad walked up to the podium in the middle of the stage. Staring into the camera, he slowly exhaled. "My people," he started, but quickly stopped and turned to face Mom and me. I took her hand, worried he would change his mind. As scared as I was to take his place, backing out now would feel like failing.

He gazed at the two of us for a moment, his lips slowly forming a smile, then looked back into the camera.

"My beloved people, I come before you tonight to ask for your mercy. In twenty years as king I have done my best to alleviate the wars and issues that threatened our peace for so long. We have formed new alliances, gotten rid of archaic social practices, and done all we can to give you, the individual, the greatest chance at personal happiness. Now, I pray you will do the same for me.

"With my wife's recent health scare, I find myself unable to focus on moving our country forward, let alone maintaining what we currently have. As such, after much thought and discussion, our family has decided that my daughter, Princess Eadlyn Schreave, will ascend the throne."

He paused to let the words sink in, and in that moment I heard the most unexpected sound: applause.

I looked up and saw it was the boys. They were clapping for me. Kile jumped to his feet, thrilled at the news, and Hale joined him, thrusting his fingers into his mouth to give a whistle. After the Elite were all standing, I realized that everyone in the studio had joined in. And not just Miss Marlee and General Leger, but the makeup girls and the floor runners who made sure the show went on without a hitch.

My lip trembled a little, completely overwhelmed by their instant joy. It bolstered my confidence. Maybe we'd been worried for nothing.

Dad, encouraged by the response, carried on as the noise died down. "We are settling plans for the coronation as we speak, and it will take place by the end of next week. Having worked side by side with the princess for the whole of her life, I know our country could not be in better hands. I also must tell you that she volunteered to take on this role early, so that her mother and I may step back from leading and enjoy simply being a husband and wife, a life we have not yet been privileged to lead. I hope you will join me in rejoicing over this wonderful news. Our whole family thanks you, our people, for your enduring support."

As soon as Dad finished speaking, the clapping and whistling started all over again. We passed each other as I went to the podium, and when he raised his hand for a high five, I couldn't not respond. I stopped in front of the podium, feeling a thousand butterflies in my stomach.

"I want to thank everyone in the palace for their help and guidance since I became regent, and let all Illéa know how delighted I am to ascend the throne. I cannot begin to express what joy it brings me to be able to do this for my parents." That was truer than anything I knew. All the nerves in the world couldn't dampen it. "And as I step into the position of queen, that means that one of these gentlemen back here won't simply be a prince. He will immediately become a prince consort."

I looked over my shoulder at them, and while some, like Fox and Kile, seemed ecstatic, Hale was frowning. So the other night wasn't just a fluke. He was having genuine doubts. What had happened? How had I lost him?

"My upcoming coronation will be one of the biggest celebrations the palace has ever seen. Please go to your Provincial Services Office for information, as one family from each province will be invited to the palace, all expenses paid, to enjoy the festivities." That had been my idea, one I felt sure Marid would appreciate. "And, of course, we appreciate your support of our family through this transitional period. We thank you, Illéa. Good night!"

I went over to Mom and Dad the second the cameras went down. "Can you believe that?"

"It went so well!" Mom said. "The boys clapping, starting it all themselves. It was so organic, and I know that had to encourage people at home."

"It's a good sign," Dad agreed. "And I think the element of your chosen husband immediately becoming a prince consort definitely adds something to this Selection."

"As if it wasn't crazy enough." I sighed and smiled, feeling too happy to care that this was all complete madness.

Dad kissed my forehead. "You were wonderful. Now, do you need some rest?" he asked, turning to Mom.

"I'm fine." She rolled her eyes as they headed off the stage.

"Are you sure? We could have dinner brought up to our room."

"So help me, if you do that, I will throw it at you."

I laughed. It was making more and more sense that they fought through their whole Selection process.

Now I just needed to get through mine.

CHAPTER 17

I RAN DOWN TO BREAKFAST the next morning, gripping the paper in my hand. I buzzed past the guards and the Elite, plunking it down in front of Mom and Dad.

"Look," I urged, pointing to the headline.

What Do They Know That We Don't? it read, the photo beneath it a shot of the boys all standing and cheering on the *Report*.

Dad picked up the paper, popped on his glasses, and read the article aloud, though not projecting his voice for the room to hear.

"'When you think of Princess Eadlyn Schreave, the first words that come to mind might not be *congenial*, *enthusiastic*, or *beloved*. She certainly has class and beauty, and while no one could argue her intellect, one might have cause to question other traits, such as her devotion to her people. So we have to ask, what is it that these young men—indeed, these Sons of Illéa—know about her that we have missed?'"

Mom looked up at me, smiling.

"'When the five remaining gentlemen in the Selection instantly rose to their feet and applauded at the announcement of the princess's ascent, I will admit, that was not this reporter's initial reaction. I was worried. She's young. She's distant. She's not in touch with her people.

"'But if these boys, all but one of them strangers to her up until recently, immediately decide to celebrate, then there must be more to our upcoming queen than a pretty face. Recently the Elite spoke of her being considerate and engaging. Are these qualities she's had all along that merely haven't been easy to translate on screen? Is she a genuine leader, prepared to sacrifice for her people?

"'The nature of her rise to the crown would suggest the answer is yes. The king and queen are still young. They are still physically and mentally able to continue their reign. To see the princess take over early so that they can enjoy their time together as a married couple shows not only her love for her family, but her commitment to her work.'"

I could see Mom's eyes welling with tears now.

"'Only time will tell if these assumptions prove true, but I can say that my faith in the crown has been—at least temporarily—restored.'"

"Oh, honey," Mom exclaimed.

Dad passed the newspaper back to me. "Eady, this is great."

"It's the most encouraging thing to happen publicly for a

long time," I agreed with a contented sigh. "I'm trying not to get my hopes up too high, but it makes going to work today that much easier."

"I hope you're planning to take it easy this morning." Mom gave me a pointed look. "I don't want you getting burned out before you even start."

"I'd tell you I have a simple morning planned, but it'd be a lie," I admitted. "I'm off to a Finnish lesson right now. Do you have any idea how difficult it is to count in Finnish?"

Dad sipped his coffee. "I've listened to it for years. I applaud you for trying."

"Henri's very sweet," Mom commented. "Not the direction I was expecting you to go in, but he'll certainly make you smile."

"*Pfft*." Dad turned to her. "What do you know about picking husbands? Last time you tried that, you got stuck with me."

She smiled and hit his arm.

"You two are so gross, you ruin everything." I spun and headed toward the door.

"Have a great day, honey," Mom called after me, and I raised a hand in acknowledgment before pausing by Henri.

"Umm. *Lähteä*?"

He beamed. "Yes! Good, good!" He dropped his napkin by his plate and took my arm.

"Wait up!" Fox called, and Kile was right behind him. "I'm looking forward to this. I think I did pretty well last time."

"Erik's such an encouraging teacher. Though you could just be stringing together random sounds, he'd tell you 'nice try,'" Kile said with a laugh.

I nodded. "Maybe it's a Swendish thing? Poor Henri was stuck helping me last time, and he had to grab my face because I was making the shapes wrong." I mimicked the action, and Henri caught on, smiling at us. "But was he bothered? Nope."

A second after I brought it up, I remembered that Henri and I might have been on the verge of a kiss in that moment. And while I was relieved to see neither of them seemed to have noticed it, I was struck by the fact that I hadn't thought about that almost kiss at all.

When we got to the library, Erik was already in there, writing on the board.

"Good morning, Professor," I greeted, walking over him.

"Your Highness. Or do we say Majesty, now?"

"Not yet!" I exclaimed. "Just thinking about that gives me the shivers."

"Well, I'm thrilled for you. We all are. I mean, *they* all are," he corrected, nodding toward the Elite, including Hale and Ean, who were walking in behind everyone. "I didn't intend to lump myself in with them. I just get to see everyone's reactions up close."

"Don't be silly. You're part of the gang." I laughed, looking around the room. "Sometimes this feels more like a weird little club than a competition."

"You're right. But that doesn't change the fact that it is."

His somber tone drew my eyes back to his face, though he was avoiding my gaze. Instead he picked up a handful of papers and gave them to me.

"And how lucky am I to be able to say I got to help the new queen learn Finnish?" His eyes glowed with pride.

I peeked over at the others, watching them choose seats, and stepped a little closer to keep my words between the two of us.

"I'll miss you, too, you know. When it's all over. You mean as much as the others. More than some."

He shook his head. "You shouldn't say that. I'm not like them."

"You are exactly like them. As common and as elevated, Eikko."

He stilled at the sound of his given name, and, just barely, the corners of his lips hitched up into a smile.

"Hey, Eady," Kile called. "Want to be my partner?"

"Sure." I walked over to him, and Erik followed.

"We'll spend a few minutes going over what we learned last week," Erik began. "Then we'll move on to some basic conversational questions and answers. I know a few of you were studying other things, and I'm happy to help with any of that, too. For now, let's go back to the numbers."

"Okay, here we go. *Yksi, kaksi, kolme, neljä, viisi*," Kile recited proudly.

"How do you do that? I'm so jealous."

"Practice. What, you don't have a spare hour to devote to counting in Finnish?"

I laughed. "I'm taking showers at a breakneck speed these days. I miss my time. But it'll be worth it, getting Mom and Dad a chance to breathe."

"I feel weird saying I'm proud of you, but I am." He tried to suppress his grin and failed. "It's like this lets me know that I'm not falling for some figment of my imagination, that you're really as smart and selfless and determined as I've started thinking you are."

"As opposed to Eadlyn circa this time last year?" I said slyly.

"Don't get me wrong, she was a fun girl. Knew how to party, knew how to light up a room. This girl does that and a hundred things more. And I like her. But you already know that."

"I like you, too," I whispered. I caught sight of Erik out of the corner of my eye and turned back to the paper. "Eight and nine trip me up because they're similar but really different at the same time."

"Okay. Let's look at those again then."

Erik walked away, and I felt guilty for wasting this class time when it was something I genuinely wanted to learn.

"Speaking of liking you, I'm sorry I haven't been able to make much time."

Kile shrugged. "Don't worry about me, Eady. I'm still here." With that he pointed to the paper in front of me, forcing me to focus on the syllables. I watched him exaggerate the shapes of the words with his mouth, all the while feeling grateful for language and time and everything waiting on my horizon.

I pushed open the office door to find Lady Brice on the phone. She waved at me as she continued speaking.

"Yes . . . yes . . . one week from today. Thank you!" She plunked down the receiver. "Sorry. Your desk is the biggest, and with the coronation in a week, there's a lot to take care of. Flowers are ready, the church is booked, we have three designers working on dress options; and if you want Neena to oversee any of that, I'm sure she'd be thrilled."

I stared at the piles of folders she'd set out. "Did you do all this in a day?"

"More or less."

I made a face at her, and she grinned before confessing the truth.

"I had a feeling it was coming, so I had a few things hammered out just in case."

I shook my head. "You know me better than I know myself."

"Part of the job. Side note," she said. "I got a call this morning from Marid. He thanked you for his family's invitation to the coronation but wasn't sure his parents would be completely welcome."

"I spoke with Dad. He knew that, right?"

"He did."

I sighed. "But Marid's coming?"

"Yes. And once this has all passed and you're settled in as queen, you can keep reaching out to them if you want."

I nodded. "If that's a bridge that can be mended, I want it done."

"That seems very wise."

I took a deep breath, basking in the praise. I'd need to keep the kind words I received close to me, like armor, if I was going to survive.

"I'm ready to work. Hit me with it."

"Actually, I think the best use of your time might be to speak with some of the Elite, or go on a date or something."

"I was just with them," I protested. "They're all fine."

"I mean more in the one-on-one sense. Besides the coronation details, which you shouldn't even be bothered with, there's nothing that can't wait until Monday. Your professional life is moving forward, and you were the one who said that it went hand in hand with your private life." She raised her eyebrows at me.

"Okay."

"Why so glum? If I remember correctly, you think all five of them are front-runners."

"It's complicated. The one I most need to talk to might not even want to speak to me." I sighed. "Wish me luck."

"You don't need it."

CHAPTER 18

I SAT IN MY ROOM, waiting for Hale to arrive. I wanted to have this conversation in a place that was intimate and comfortable. My palms were sweating, and I realized rather abruptly I was getting down to the boys I really didn't want to send home. I knew only one would stay in the end, but I almost wished the others could call the palace home, too, or maybe promise to visit on holidays.

I snapped my head up at the knock on the door and went to answer it myself. I didn't want Eloise around for this.

Hale bowed. "Your Highness."

"Come in. Are you hungry? Thirsty?"

"No, I'm good." He rubbed his hands together, looking as nervous as I was.

I sat at the table, and he joined me.

When I couldn't bear the silence any longer, I spoke. "I

need you to tell me what's going on."

He swallowed. "And I want to tell you. But I don't know what I'll do if you end up hating me because of it."

Despite the warmth, I felt a chill. "Why would I hate you, Hale? What did you do?"

"It's not something I did. It's something I can't do."

"Which is?"

"Marry you."

Though I'd been expecting as much, though my heart had never really, fully been his, it was still a painful blow.

"What—" I had to stop and breathe. This was my worst fear coming to life. I was unlovable. I knew it. All it had taken was a few weeks by my side for him to figure it out. "What suddenly made you so certain you couldn't marry me?"

He paused, looking pained, and I took some consolation in the fact that he didn't seem to *want* to hurt me. "When I found I had feelings for someone else."

At least that was easier to handle than my initial worry. "Carrie?"

He shook his head. "Ean."

I was driven to absolute silence. Ean? Like, *Ean* Ean?

I didn't see that coming. Hale had been so tender, so romantic. But instantly everything about Ean became clear.

When the castes had been in place, it was law that every family fell into the caste of the husband. Because of that, there could only ever be one male head of the household. The same went for women: no married couple, no legitimate household. Some people lived together without bothering with marriage, calling their lovers roommates, but it was frowned on. Mom told me about a same-sex couple back in Carolina who'd been shunned to the point that they were driven out of town.

I'd never cared for that story. It sounded to me like way too many people had it hard when she was growing up. Why would anyone go out of their way to make someone's life any harder?

Regardless, same-sex couples tended to live in the shadows, on the outskirts of society, and unfortunately that was still the case today. This made Ean's acceptance of not finding love in his life much more understandable.

But Hale?

"How . . . how did you even . . . ?"

"We started talking one night in the Men's Parlor. I hadn't been able to sleep and decided to go there to read. I found him writing in his journal." Hale smiled to himself. "You wouldn't think it to look at him, but he's actually very poetic.

"Anyway, we just talked. And, I don't know how we even got to the point where we were sitting beside each other, but then he kissed me, and . . . I knew why I never had a crush on Carrie. I knew why, even though you are the smartest, funniest, bravest girl I know, I couldn't marry you."

I closed my eyes, taking this in. And I felt absolutely horrified, because all that came to my mind was how badly this might affect me. Forget that Hale was going to have to explain this discovery about himself to his family, forget that

Ean might finally be forced to come clean. What would the press say when they eventually learned that not one but two of my suitors would rather be with each other than with me?

Sometimes I was a really terrible person.

"I know that a Selected being in a relationship with someone else is treason," Hale breathed. I raised my eyes, having forgotten that detail. "But I also know that a short, honest life is better than a long, deceitful one."

"Hale," I urged, leaning across the table to take his hand. "What makes you think I could even punish you?"

"I know the rules."

I sighed. "We live our lives bound by them, don't we?"

He nodded.

"Perhaps you and I could make a deal?"

"What kind of deal?"

I pulled my hands back, rubbing them together. "If you would do me the favor of staying until after the coronation and letting me dismiss you and Ean a few weeks, or maybe even days, apart, then I will allow you to leave the palace without any sort of repercussions."

He stared at me. "Really?"

"I admit, I'm worried about the fallout from all this. But if it looks like you two fell for each other after you were eliminated, then no one could accuse you of treason. And, I'm sorry, but if the press found out, they'd tear me apart over this."

"I really didn't want to make things harder for you. I'm

not in love with you, but I love you enough to tell you the truth."

Standing, I bridged the space between us. He stood, too, and I flung my arms around him, resting my head on his shoulder. "I know. And I love you, too. I wouldn't wish you a lifetime shackled to me when it would make you miserable."

"Is there anything I can do for you? Leaving here with your blessing was more than I hoped for. How can I help you?"

I stepped back. "Just be an exemplary Selection candidate for a few more days. I realize that's asking a lot, but getting me past the coronation would mean the world to me."

"It's not asking a lot, Eadlyn. It's hardly asking anything."

I put a hand on his cheek. Something every day.

"So, is he the one or what?"

Hale laughed, the relief finally hitting him. "I don't know. I mean, I've never felt like this before."

I nodded. "Since he and I don't talk much, maybe you'd like to tell him how your eliminations will work? He'll probably go home before you, since publicly he looked like a less likely candidate."

Saying that out loud caused a little ping in my chest, too. Ean had been a safety net; and still, knowing the truth, I didn't relish the idea of him going home.

"Thank you. For all of this."

"Don't mention it."

Hale swept in and hugged me again before running off. I smiled, thinking that Hale and I were in very similar situations: charging headlong into the future with no guarantee of a happily ever after. All the same, it meant something that we ran, didn't it?

I liked to think so.

The day had gone from wonderful to complicated very quickly, and by the end of it I was ready to bypass dinner and fall straight into bed. I pushed my door open, trying to hold on to the best parts of the day. Lady Brice saying I was wise. The press feeling hopeful. Hale's smile before he ran out of the room.

"You know," a deep voice said, "I think I might be your maid's favorite."

Kile was lounging on my bed, his arms comfortably crossed behind his head.

I laughed. "And why is that?"

"Because she was far too easy to bribe."

"The least you could have done was take off your shoes."

He made a face and slipped them off, then patted the space on the bed beside him.

I flopped down, looking incredibly unladylike. He rolled over, facing me, and I caught a glimpse of his fingers. "What in the world have you been doing today?"

"I spent the afternoon sketching with charcoals," he answered, flipping his blackened hands over. "Don't worry. They won't rub off on your sheets. My fingers are just stained."

"What'd you dream up?"

"I realize this might be overstepping boundaries, but I was thinking about the town hall, and I was wondering if it might be helpful to have things like that more often. I was redesigning one of the parlors into a permanent throne room, where you could receive people, hear individual petitions, and address them one-on-one. Something official but understated."

"That's really thoughtful."

He shrugged. "I told you, I keep making things for you."

The glimmer in his eyes was so boyish that for a moment I forgot we were on the verge of so many grown-up things.

"You also might want to think about setting up a radio station," he commented.

"Ugh, why? The *Reports* are bad enough."

"When I was taking classes in Fennley, my friends and I listened to the radio a lot. We would leave it on in the kitchen or while we worked, and any time we heard something interesting, we'd stop and listen and start our own discussion. It might be a good way for you to reach people. And it's not quite as bad as having a camera in your face."

"Interesting. I'll think about it." I touched the tips of his dirty fingers. "Did you work on anything else?"

He made a face. "Remember those little units I was talking about? I was trying to see if they could be built with an upstairs, for larger families. But looking at the materials I wanted to use, it doesn't seem possible. The metal would be too thin. It would be helpful if I could actually build one and test it out. Maybe one day."

I stared at him. "You know, Kile, princes rarely get their hands dirty."

"I know." He smiled. "It's more something nice to think about than anything." He shifted his weight and the conversation in one swift movement. "The papers looked good today."

"Yeah. Now I just have to keep that momentum going. I have no idea how to re-create it though."

"You don't have to. Sometimes things just happen."

"It would feel nice to not try to *work* at it all so much." I yawned. Even a mostly good day was tiring.

"Do you want me to go so that you can get some rest?"

"Nah," I said, settling in a little closer and rolling onto my back. "Can you stay here for a little while?"

"Sure."

He held my hand, and we stared at the intricate painting on my ceiling.

"Eadlyn?"

"Yeah."

"You okay?"

"Yeah. I feel like I'd be doing better if I could go slower, but everything has to be now, now, now."

"You could push the coronation back. Stay regent for a while. It's practically the same thing."

"I know, but it doesn't feel the same. My dad was doing okay with me as regent, but even in the short time since we set a date for the coronation, he's been much better. I know it's all mental, but if it helps him sleep, which helps him with Mom, which helps her get better . . ."

"I see what you're saying. But what else? You're not rushing through the Selection, are you?"

"Not on purpose. It seems to be thinning itself out for me."

"What do you mean?"

I sighed. "I can't really say now. Maybe once everything's settled."

"You can trust me."

"I know." I leaned my head into his shoulder. "Kile?"

"Yeah."

"Do you remember our first kiss?"

"How could I forget? It was printed on the front of every newspaper."

"No, not that one. Our *first* first kiss."

After a beat of confusion, he sucked in a huge breath. "Oh. My. Gosh."

I just lay there laughing.

When I was four and Kile was six, he and I played together a lot. I still didn't remember what made him start hating palace life or when our mutual dislike for each other kicked in, but back then Kile was like another Ahren. One day the three of us were playing hide-and-seek, and Kile found me. Instead of tagging me out, though, he bent down and kissed me full on the mouth.

I stood up and pushed him to the ground and swore to him that if he ever tried it again, I'd have him hanged.

"What four-year-old knows how to threaten someone's life?" he teased.

"One who was raised to, I suppose."

"Wait, is this your way of telling me you're having me hanged? Because, if so, this is incredibly cold."

"No." I laughed. "I felt you deserved an apology by now."

"It's fine. Really funny years later. When people ask about my first kiss, I never say that one. I tell them it was the daughter of the Saudi prime minister. I guess that one was actually my second."

"Why don't you tell them about me?"

"Because I thought you might follow through on the hanging thing," he joked. "I guess I just blocked it out. It wasn't exactly a fantastic first kiss."

I started giggling. "Mom told me that she was Dad's first kiss, and she pretty much tried to back out of it."

"Really?!"

"Yeah."

Kile laughed. "Do you know about Ahren's?"

"No." But Kile was so tickled, I was in tears before he said a word.

"It was with one of the Italian girls, but he had a cold and—" He paused because he was laughing so hard. "Oh, man, he had to sneeze mid-kiss, so there was snot everywhere."

"What?"

"I didn't see the kiss, but I was there for the aftermath. I just grabbed him, and we ran."

My stomach hurt from laughing, and it took a while for it to wear out of our systems. When we finally calmed down, I realized something. "I don't know anyone who's had a really good first kiss."

After a second he answered. "Me neither. Maybe it's not the first kisses that are supposed to be special. Maybe it's the last ones."

CHAPTER 19

I STOOD STILL AS NEENA placed pins down the back of my coronation gown. It was a showstopper, with a sweetheart neckline and a full skirt all in gold. The cape was a little heavy, but I only had to wear that in the church. While I had chosen this gown out of the three that had been offered to me, it probably wasn't what I'd have worn if I'd had time to design the dress myself. Still, everyone sighed when they saw it, so I bit my tongue and was grateful.

"You look beautiful, darling," Mom said as I stood on a raised platform in front of huge mirrors that had been brought to my room especially for this fitting.

"Thanks, Mom. How do you think it compares with yours?"

She chuckled. "My coronation dress was also my wedding

dress, so there's no comparison. Your gown is perfect for the occasion."

Neena chuckled as I touched the embroidery on the bodice. "It's definitely the most ostentatious dress I've ever worn."

"And just think, you'll have to one-up yourself when you get married," Neena joked.

My smile faded. "True. That'll be a challenge, huh?"

"You okay?" she asked, looking at me in the mirror.

"Yes. A little tired is all."

"I don't care what else happens this week, you need to rest," Mom ordered. "Saturday is going to be long, and you'll be at the center of it all."

"Yes, ma'am." I watched her fiddling with her necklace. "Mom? What do you think you would have done if you couldn't have married Dad? Like, if it got to the end and he chose someone else?"

She shook her head. "He very nearly did. You know about the massacre." She swallowed, pausing for a minute. After all this time it was still hard for her to go back there. "That day he might have gone down an entirely different path, which meant I would have, too."

"Would you have been okay though?"

"Eventually," she said slowly. "I don't think either of us would have lived a life that was bad necessarily. It just might not have been the best it could have been."

"But you wouldn't have been completely miserable the rest of your life?"

She studied my face in the mirror. "If you're worried about letting your suitors down, you can't focus on that."

I pressed my hands to my stomach, holding the dress tight as Neena worked. "I know. It's just harder than I thought it would be by this point."

"It'll become clear. Trust me. And your father and I will support you in whatever choice you make."

"Thank you."

"I think this is finally coming together," Neena commented, stepping back to appraise her work. "If you're happy, you can take it off, and I'll have the courier send it back to Allmond."

Mom nibbled on some apple slices. "I don't understand why he wouldn't let you do the sewing. He trusts you to fit it."

She shrugged. "I just follow orders."

A quiet knock on the door drew our attention. "Come in," Neena called, falling into her old role. I wished she could just run my entire life for me. Everything felt easier with her around.

A butler entered and bowed. "Pardon me, Your Highness. There's some confusion about the suit for one of the gentlemen."

"Which one?"

"Erik, miss."

"The translator?" Mom asked.

"Yes, Your Majesty."

"I'm coming," I said, following him out the door.

"Don't you want to take off the gown?" Neena asked.

"It'll give me a chance to practice walking in it."

And it did. It was incredibly heavy, and a little hard to navigate down the stairs. I'd need sturdier heels.

As I approached Erik's room, I could hear him imploring someone to reconsider. "I am not an Elite. It would be inappropriate."

I pushed the door open wider, finding him in a suit with chalk lines down the sides and pins in the hem.

"Your Highness," the tailor said, immediately dropping into a bow.

Erik, however, stared and stared, unable to look away from the dress.

"We're having a problem coming to terms with his suit, miss." The tailor motioned to the chalked-up suit.

Erik regained his composure. "I don't want to confuse anyone by wearing a suit that matches what the Elite are wearing."

"But you will be walking in the procession, and there will be scores of pictures," the tailor insisted. "Uniformity is best."

Erik looked at me, his eyes pleading.

I pressed my fingers to my lips, considering. "Could you give us a moment, please?"

The tailor bowed again and exited, and I crossed to stand in front of Erik.

"It does look rather sharp," I said with a grin.

"It does," he admitted. "I'm just not sure it's proper."

"What? To look nice for a day?"

"I'm not an Elite. It's . . . confusing to have me standing with them, looking like them, when I can't . . . I'm not . . ."

I put a hand on his chest. "The tailor is right. You will want to blend in. A different color of suit wouldn't help your case here."

He sighed. "But I'm—"

"What if your tie was a slightly different color?" I offered quickly.

"Is that my only option?"

"Yes. Besides, think of how much your mother will love this."

He rolled his eyes. "That's so unfair. You win."

I clapped my hands. "See? That wasn't so hard."

"Of course it was easy for you. You were the one giving the command."

"I didn't mean to command you, not really."

He smirked. "Of course you did. You're made for it."

I couldn't tell if that was a critique or a compliment. "What do you think?" I asked, holding out my arms. "I mean, you have to try to imagine it without all the pins."

He paused. "You look breathtaking, Eadlyn. I couldn't even remember what I was so worked up about when you first walked in."

I fought the blush. "I've been wondering if it was too much."

"It's perfect. I can see it's a little different from your usual style, but then again, your typical look isn't meant to be coronation-day ready."

I turned around and looked in the mirror. That one sentence made the whole thing so much better.

"Thank you. I think I've been overanalyzing it."

He stood beside me. It was comical, these beautiful clothes, some of the best we'd ever wear, marked in chalk and held by pins. We looked like dolls. "That seems to be a talent of yours."

I grimaced but nodded. He was right.

"I realize I'm in no position to tell you what to do," he said, "but you seem to handle things much better when you think about them less. Get out of your head. Trust your gut. Trust your heart."

"I'm terrified of my heart." I didn't mean to say those words out loud, but there was something about him that made this room, and this moment, the only place I could ever admit to the truth.

He leaned down by my ear and whispered, "There's nothing there to fear." He cleared his throat, then turned back to face our reflections. "Maybe what you need is a little luck. You see this ring?" he asked, holding out his pinkie.

I did. I'd noticed it a dozen times. Why would someone who dulled himself down and refused to put on a suit wear a piece of jewelry?

"This was my great-great-grandmother's wedding ring. The weaving design is a traditional Swendish thing. You see it everywhere in Swendway." He slipped off the ring and held it between two fingers. "This has survived everything from wars to famine, even my family's move to Illéa. I'm supposed to give it to the girl I marry. Mom's orders."

I smiled, charmed by his excitement. I wondered if there was someone back home hoping to wear it someday.

"But it seems to have a lot of good luck," he continued. "I think you could use some right now."

He held out the ring to me, but I shook my head. "I can't take that! It's an heirloom."

"Yes, but it's a very fortunate heirloom. It's guided several people to their soul mates. And it's only temporary. Until you get to the end of the Selection, or Henri and I leave. Whichever happens first."

Hesitantly, I slid the ring onto my finger, noting how smooth it was.

"Thank you, Erik."

I looked into his blue eyes. It only took one charged second to hear the heart that I'd had so little faith in. It was taking in that piercing stare and the warm scent of his skin . . . and it was shouting.

Without considering the repercussions or the complications, without knowing if he felt anything similar to what I did, I leaned into him. And I was thrilled to find he wasn't pulling away. We were so close I could feel his breath across my lips.

"Have we made a decision?" the tailor asked, springing back in.

I jerked away from Erik. "Yes. Please finish the suit for us, sir."

Without looking back, I hurried into the hallway. My heart was racing as I found an empty guest room and darted inside, slamming the door behind me.

I had felt it growing, this feeling that had been hiding beneath the surface for some time now. I'd seen him, this person who never intended to be seen, and my faulty, silly, useless heart kept whispering his name. I clutched my chest, feeling my heart racing. "You treacherous, treacherous thing. What have you done?"

I'd wondered how it was possible to magically find a soul mate in a random group of boys.

But now I couldn't question it.

CHAPTER 20

THE NEXT FEW DAYS PASSED in a whirlwind of preparation for the coronation. I did my absolute best to stay in my office and take meals in my room, but even so, I couldn't avoid Erik completely.

We had to go by the church and practice the procession, in which he was forced to participate in order to even out the number of people walking behind me. And he had to stick by Henri as we walked the Elite through the Great Room, explaining how best to circulate at a formal party. And I had to approve the final fitting of their suits, which I managed to do without making eye contact but which still was much, much harder than I'd have thought.

The coronation would be one of the most important moments of my life, and still, all I could think about was how it might have felt to kiss him.

★ ★ ★

I was running late. I never ran late.

But my hair wouldn't curl the right way, and a seam popped under my arm, and though I'd picked out sensible heels earlier in the week, once I tried them on with the dress, I hated them.

Eloise took deep breaths as she got my hair right, practicing with a mock crown to check that everything would look as beautiful as possible when the actual moment arrived. Neena was busy making sure people were dressed and ready, so it was Hale who dashed in at the last moment with a needle and thread to make sure everything with the dress was fixed.

"Thank you," I breathed.

He tied off the last stitch. "Any time." He looked at his watch. "Though I really wish you'd have asked earlier."

"It didn't pop until I put it on!"

He smiled. "I gave everything a once-over, and it looks like that was the only weak spot. Better we caught it now than in the middle of the day."

I nodded. "I need things to be perfect today. Just once I'd like to come across as put together but not so put together that I hate everything and everyone around me."

Hale laughed. "Well then, if it happens to pop again, roll with it."

Eloise went to fetch something from the bathroom, and I took my chance. "How's Ean?" I asked in a whisper.

"Good. Stunned," he answered, almost giddy. "We both

want to help you in whatever way we can. You're making our futures possible, so we owe you one."

"Just help me get through today, and that will be plenty."

"Something every day," he reminded me.

I hopped off the pedestal and hugged him. "You've been incredibly worthy."

"That's good to know," he replied, returning my embrace. "Okay, I'm getting my suit jacket and heading downstairs. Let me know if you need me today."

I nodded, trying not to tense as Eloise came back to do her final touch-ups.

"He's a nice one," she remarked, spraying the last of the flyaways.

"He is."

"Personally, I'd pick Kile," she commented with a giggle.

"I know!" I shook my head at her. "I still haven't forgotten how you let him sneak into my room."

She shrugged. "He is my favorite. I have to do what I can!"

Finally everything was in place. I made my way downstairs, the tail of my cape draped over my arm. The foyer was a mass of people. General Leger on one side holding Miss Lucy's hands to his lips, Josie and Neena in matching pale-blue gowns that would look lovely as they held my train down the aisle, and the five remaining Elite in a circle toward a corner, with Erik wearing a tie that was a shade of blue slightly brighter than the others.

But I only had eyes for one boy in the crowd. As I reached

the middle of the staircase, I caught sight of Ahren. He was here.

I rushed through the herd, elbowing my way past advisers and friends, running not into Ahren's arms, but Camille's.

"Is he well?" I asked into her ear.

"*Oui*, very."

"And are your people pleased? Do they accept him?"

"As if he was born one of our own."

I held her tighter. "Thank you."

I pulled away, turning to see my stupid brother.

"You clean up nice," he teased.

I didn't know if I should joke with him or punch him in the arm or scream or laugh or anything at all. So I crushed him in a hug.

"I'm sorry," he whispered. "I shouldn't have left the way I did. I shouldn't have left you alone."

I shook my head. "You were right. I miss you so much it hurts, but you had to go."

"As soon as I heard about Mom, I wanted to come back. But I didn't know if it would make things worse or better, or if it was even fair for me to show up since it seemed I was the cause."

"Don't be ridiculous. All that matters is that you're here now."

He held me close for a minute as Lady Brice organized everyone into cars. The advisers went first and the Elite just after, all of them bowing deeply to me, Erik especially. He didn't meet my eyes, and I was grateful. Who knew what my stupid heart might have done if he had?

It did melt a little when he walked away, pulling repeatedly at his sleeves, seeming painfully uncomfortable in his suit.

"Okay, next car," Lady Brice announced. "Everyone whose last name is Schreave, even you, Monsieur French Prince."

"Yes, ma'am," Ahren said, taking Camille's hand.

"Eadlyn's in first, followed by Neena and Josie. The rest of the family in after that, and I'll be in a car right behind you."

Dad paused. "Brice, you should be with us."

"Absolutely," Mom agreed. "There's room in the limo, and you're the one holding this whole thing together."

"I'm not sure that's appropriate," she replied.

Neena tilted her head, trying to put doubt in Lady Brice's mind. "It could easily fall apart on the ten-minute drive."

"Also, the likelihood of someone thinking Neena and I are sisters is slim," I added. "Stay with us."

She pursed her lips as if she thought this was somehow a bad idea. "Fine. Let's go."

We piled into the limo, my dress taking up the space of three people. There was so much laughter and feet stepping over feet that the whole thing started to feel funny. I took a deep breath. All I had to do was say a few words, make a promise I'd already made in my heart. I looked across the car to Mom. She gave me a wink, and that was all I needed.

★ ★ ★

Josie and Neena followed me down the aisle of the church, holding my cape so it didn't drag across the floor. As I walked, I looked at the signet ring on my finger, the Illéan crest gleaming in the center. Dad already trusted me in this role. He was already delighted with the way I was handling it. This was just making everything official.

I caught the eyes of as many people as I could, hoping to convey my gratitude. At the head of the church, I knelt on the little resting stool, feeling the weight of my dress fanned out behind me. The bishop took the ceremonial crown and held it above my head.

"Are you, Eadlyn Schreave, willing to take this oath?"

"I am willing."

"Do you vow to uphold the laws and honor of Illéa all the days of your life, governing your people according to their traditions and customs?"

"I do."

"And do you vow to protect the interests of Illéa, both at home and abroad?"

"I do."

"And do you vow to use your power and placement to bring mercy and justice for all Illéa's people?"

"I do."

It felt appropriate that vows to a country required four affirmations, whereas vows to another person only required one. With my final words spoken, the bishop set the crown on my head. I rose and turned to face my people, my cape looking rather beautiful curled up around my feet like a cat. The bishop placed the scepter in my left hand and the orb in my right.

There was a loud knock of a staff on the floor, and the people around me shouted, "God save the queen."

And I felt a thrill in my chest to know those words were meant for me.

CHAPTER 21

"OSTEN, FOR GOODNESS' SAKE, STAND up," Mom ordered.

"But it's so hot," he complained as we began what would be a marathon photo session.

Dad stepped around me. "You can pull it together for five minutes of pictures, son."

Ahren laughed. "Oh, I've missed you all."

I swatted him. "I'm so glad no one's actually filming this."

"Okay, okay. We're all ready," Dad called to the photographer. He and Mom posed behind me, their arms on the back of my chair. Osten and Ahren knelt on either side of me, while Kaden stood with one hand behind his back, almost challenging me for the most regal-looking family member of the day.

The photographer snapped shot after shot until he was satisfied. "And who's next?"

We all stayed where we were, pulling Camille into the picture. Then, so we would have a picture of the whole family, each of the Elite boys was rotated through the portrait.

Then it was a picture of me with the Legers, then one with each member of the advisory board, including Lady Brice, who bypassed the traditionally stiff pose and hugged me tightly instead. "I'm so proud!" she kept saying. "Just so, so proud!" Then, of course, we had to get a shot with the entire Woodwork family.

Josie walked up as fast as she could, placing herself so she was practically front and center. I shook my head as Miss Marlee gave me a big hug.

"I'm so happy for you, honey. You've grown up so fast."

I laughed. "Thank you, Miss Marlee. I'm glad you could all be here today."

Mr. Woodwork smiled. "As if we'd miss it. Congratulations."

Miss Marlee still held my hands. "These past few months, seeing you ascend, and watching you and Kile become so close, have been wonderful."

I smiled. "Honestly, it's hard to imagine us not being friends now. I can't believe it took us this long to actually get to know each other."

"It's funny how that works," Miss Marlee replied. "It seems like a shame you and Josie have hardly gotten to spend any time together."

"What?" Josie said, able to hear her name if it was so much as tapped out in Morse code on a different continent.

"It might be good for you to do more together." Miss Marlee looked between the two of us, glowing with joy.

"Yeah! We totally should!" Josie squealed.

"And I'd love to," I lied. "But now that I'm queen, I'm afraid my free time will be very limited."

Mom smiled knowingly behind her friend. I could tell she realized exactly what I was trying to do.

Miss Marlee frowned. "True. Oh, I know! Why don't you have Josie shadow you for a few days? She's always had a deep interest in the life of a princess. Now she can study a queen!"

"That. Would be. Amazing!" Josie grabbed my hand, and to my credit, I didn't jerk it away.

With everyone waiting for me to speak and my mother's eyes warning me that, queen or not, I'd better not disappoint her closest friend, I didn't have a choice.

"Sure. Josie can shadow me. That will be . . . great."

Josie danced back to her spot, and I eyed Kile, who was doing his best not to laugh at my newest predicament. His amusement made me smile, and I felt confident that I'd at least look happy in the pictures.

Finally it was time for the individual portraits with the Elite. I stood in my coronation gown as they were each cycled onto the set.

Fox was first, and he looked sharp in his dark-gray suit. "Okay, so what do I do?" he asked. "In the family picture, I put my arms by my side; but I feel like I should, I don't know, hold your hand or something."

The photographer called out, "Yes, that's good," as Fox

took my hand in his. He stepped a little closer, and we smiled as clicks flashed through in quick succession.

Ean sauntered over next, looking quite pleased. "Stunning, Eadlyn. Absolutely stunning."

"Thanks. You don't look so bad yourself."

"True," he said, smirking. "Very true."

He positioned himself behind me. "I haven't gotten to thank you yet. Both for your pardon and your discretion."

"You and I always got by on minimal communication. I knew you were thankful."

"I'd been preparing myself for a life of disappointment," he admitted, his tone the closest to nervousness I'd ever heard it. "To consider that anything else is possible feels unreal. I'm not quite sure how to move forward."

"Just live."

Ean smiled at me, kissed my forehead, and moved to the side.

After Ean it was Kile's turn, and he barreled across the set, making me scream when he scooped me up and spun me around.

"Put me down!"

"Why? Because you're queen? I'll need a better reason than that."

He finally stopped, facing the camera, and I knew we were both grinning like idiots. These pictures would be a completely different kind of spectacular.

"I nearly killed myself stepping on that cape," he said. "Fashion is deadly."

"Don't say that to Hale," I commented.

"Say what to me?" Hale said as they switched places.

"That fashion can kill." Kile straightened his suit as he walked.

"Hers could. You look amazing," he said, embracing me.

"Thanks so much for your help this morning. Everything held together."

"Of course it did. Did you doubt my skills?" he teased.

"Never."

I stood back so we could take a few pictures with our faces showing, though I couldn't wait to see the ones of us embracing.

Finally it was Henri's turn, and his smile alone was enough to make this long day feel short. He stopped a few steps away from me and took a deep breath.

"You are look very beautiful. I am happy for you."

My hand flew to my mouth, so moved. "Henri. Thank you! Thank you so much!"

He shrugged. "I trying."

"You're doing great. Really."

He nodded and came over to me, gently turning me away from him. Then he walked around to move my cape so it fluttered around from behind me, and he came to the other side, placing his hands on my waist, standing proudly just over my shoulder.

It was clear he had put a lot of thought into how he wanted to be perceived in this portrait, and I admired that. When the photographer was done, Henri began to walk away, then paused.

"Umm, *entä* Erik?" he said, pointing to his friend.

Kile caught on and was in full agreement. "Yeah, Erik's been through this, too. He needs to get up there."

Erik simply shook his head. "No, I'm fine. It's fine."

"Go on, man, it's just a picture." Kile pushed him a little, but he still didn't move.

Part of me worried that somehow, everyone would be able to hear my pulse beating out his name if he got any closer. But as hard as I'd worked to avoid him the last few days, it was just as challenging not to run to him now.

I walked over to him. And when he realized I was on my way, his gaze flew up to mine. In an instant, everything in the room came alive. Like the sunshine had a melody and the sounds of footsteps had a texture I could feel in my fingertips each time anyone moved.

The world woke up when I looked at him.

I stopped in front of Erik, hoping I didn't look as dazzled as I felt. "I'm not commanding. I'm asking."

He sighed. "That makes it a thousand times worse." Smiling, he put his hand in mine, but before I could pull him onto the stage, he looked down at himself. As soon as the ceremony had ended, he'd taken off his suit jacket and was now only wearing a vest and tie. "Now I'm underdressed," he lamented.

I sighed and unbuttoned the snaps holding the cape to my dress. The second I held it out, Hale came to carefully take it away. "Does that help?"

"No." He swallowed. "But if you truly want this . . ."

"I do." I tilted my head and playfully batted my lashes.

He laughed, clearly realizing he was defeated. "What do I do?"

"Okay." I grinned, stepping closer. "Put this hand here," I said, placing the front one on my waist. "And this one here," pulling the other up to my shoulder. I put one hand on his chest and the other looped behind his arm, and we stood there in a loose embrace. "Now smile at the camera."

"All right," he said.

With my hand on his chest, I could feel his heart pounding. "Calm down," I said quietly. "Pretend it's just you and me."

"I can't."

"Then, I don't know, say something in Finnish."

He chuckled to himself and whispered, "*Vain koska pyysit, hauska nainen.*" Though I couldn't understand the words he continued to murmur, I knew I would never be able to forget his tone. Without looking up at him, I could hear his smile, which only made mine brighter. I had to remind myself to breathe, I was so busy listening to him. I knew in my heart these were important words. And I couldn't recognize a single one.

"That was a good one," the photographer said, and almost instantly Erik dropped his hands.

"See? Was that so awful?" I asked.

"I thought it would be much, much harder," he confessed, and there was something funny in his voice, like I'd missed a detail.

I could hear it again, the *rat tat tat* of my foolish heart. I swallowed, ignoring it and turning instead to the footsteps echoing as they entered the hall.

"Marid," I called in greeting.

"I'm sorry to intrude, but I couldn't help myself. Is there any way I could get an official picture with my new queen?" Marid asked.

"Of course." I extended a hand, and he walked over, happily taking it.

"The country is abuzz," he told me. "I don't know if you've been hearing reports today, but the coverage is very positive."

"I haven't had a second to pause and look," I confessed as he held both of my hands affectionately and faced the camera.

"No need. You have people at your beck and call to report it all later. I'm just happy to be the first to tell you that your inaugural day is going beautifully."

He squeezed my hand, and I sighed, thinking that maybe, finally, it was all coming together.

CHAPTER 22

I DRANK CHAMPAGNE AND LAUGHED too loudly and ate half my body weight in chocolate. Just for a few hours, I wanted to revel in the ridiculous opulence I'd always taken for granted. Tomorrow I would sip water and get my head straight. Tomorrow I would worry about how to keep my country together. Tomorrow I would think about husbands.

But tonight? Tonight I was going to bask in this perfect, sparkling moment.

"One more dance?" Ahren asked, catching me mid-sip in what I swore was my last drink. "I have a flight to catch, but I wanted to say good-bye."

I stood, taking his hand. "I'll take whatever good-bye I can get. Anything will be better than last time."

"I'm still sorry about that, but you know why I couldn't."

We locked form, and he spun me around the room. "I

do. That didn't make it any easier though. Add that to everything else that's going on, and life's been a little harsh without you here."

"I'm sorry. But you're doing very well, better than you think, I'd wager."

"We'll see. I still have to establish my government, make sure Mom and Dad slow down, and find someone to marry me."

He shrugged. "So, basically nothing."

"It's practically a vacation."

He chuckled. Oh, how I had missed that sound. "I'm sorry if my letter was harsh. Mom and Dad wanted to protect you, but I was afraid that not knowing where you stood might actually cripple you."

"It wasn't easy to read, but it's come up again and again. I really should have known. If I hadn't been so self-centered—"

"You were trying to shield yourself," he said quickly, cutting me off. "You are doing something no one else in this country has ever done. Of course you found ways to make it easier."

I shook my head. "Dad has been exhausted. Mom has never slowed down. You were in love, and I tried to talk you out of it. There's a word for what I am, but I'm too much of a lady to say it."

He laughed out loud at that, and I caught several eyes looking our way, most noticeably Camille's. I'd wanted to be mad at her, this girl who'd done everything I was trying to do but ten times better, this girl who'd taken away my twin.

But it was clear how happy she was to see us reunited.

I still didn't understand how she'd mastered everything so easily, how she seemed to maintain being a leader and a girl without effort. I worried that, as perfect as this day was, it wouldn't last.

"Hey," he said, noting the worry in my eyes. "It will be fine. You're going to make it through this."

I fixed my face, trying to find the magic that had been running through my veins only moments ago. I was the new queen; it wouldn't do for me to be sad on today of all days. "I know. I'm just not sure how."

The song came to a close, and Ahren bowed deeply. "You must come to Paris for New Year's."

"And you have to come back for our next birthday," I insisted.

"Then you have to honeymoon in France."

"Not unless you come back here for the wedding."

He held out a hand. "Deal."

We shook on it, and my precious twin pulled me close for a hug. "I was mourning for days, thinking you'd never forgive me for leaving. The fact that you're not mad at all makes going that much harder."

"You have to call. And not just Mom and Dad, you have to call me."

"I will."

"I love you, Ahren."

"I love you, Your Majesty."

I laughed, and we both took a moment to dab at our eyes.

"Speaking of that wedding," he started, "any idea who your groom will be?"

We surveyed the room. The Elite were easy to spot with their crisp suits and ties, as handsome as any of the visiting royalty. I'd watched them all night, adding their behavior to the piles of information I had about them.

Kile had graciously entertained most of the younger guests, and Fox had shaken so many hands I caught him massaging his wrists at one point. Though Ean and Hale were out of the running, I'd overheard them both giving glowing commentaries about my character to the press, going above and beyond anything I'd hoped for. And then there was Henri. He had done his best with Erik at his side, helping him through conversations, but as I watched him studying the partygoers from his seat, it was clear he'd had a rough time.

"I've gone back and forth a few times. It's hard to know for sure who the right choice is. I just want to do what's best for everyone."

"Including you?"

I smiled, unable to answer.

"If there's one thing I hope my leaving home proves," he said seriously, "it's that you have to do whatever it takes to be with the person you love."

Love. Like clothes, I had guessed it was something that fit no two people exactly the same way. I was still unsure what the word looked like for me, but I sensed that, sooner rather than later, it would be fully defined. All that remained to be seen was if I could be satisfied with the definition.

"I'm telling you, Eady, wars and treaties and even countries will all come and go. But your life is yours, singular and sacred, and you should be with the person who makes it feel that way every blessed second you live it."

I looked down, studying my gown, feeling the weight of the crown on my head. Yes, my life was singular and sacred, but from the moment of my birth—a mere seven minutes before his—it had belonged to anyone but me.

"Thank you, Ahren. I'll remember that."

"Please do."

I put my hand on his shoulder. "Go find your wife. Be safe getting home, and let us know when you land, okay?"

He took my hand from his sleeve and kissed it. "Bye, Eady."

"Bye."

Though I was getting tired, I knew it wasn't yet time for me to sneak away. *One last lap,* I told myself. I'd shake hands, give two or three interviews, and duck out the side door.

So many smiles and hugs, so many well wishes and promises to be in contact soon. It cycled energy through me almost as quickly as it sucked it back out. As I rounded the corner where Ean was speaking with a few people who had won the lottery to come to the coronation, another waltz started playing.

"Oh, a dance!" a young girl pleaded. I thought she meant she wanted Ean to dance with her, but she nudged him in my direction, and he was only too happy to escort me onto the floor.

After a few turns I had to ask, "How long have you liked Hale?"

He smiled. "From the moment we were getting prepped to meet you. He just looked so happy, to the point of being cartoonish. It was endearing."

"It is endearing," I agreed.

"I'm sorry I lied to you. I was planning on taking this to my grave."

"And now?"

He shrugged. "I'm not sure. But Hale's so damned insistent on being true to yourself that, at the very least, I wouldn't try to use someone like a screen to hide it, the way I tried to with you. It's not fair to anyone."

"It's hard to be fair to yourself sometimes, isn't it?"

He nodded. "I wouldn't compare our circumstances though. In the end, no one cares about me, and everyone cares about you."

"Don't be silly. I care about you. I cared about the swaggering snob who introduced himself that very first day." He laughed, thinking back. Some of that veneer had slipped away. Not all of it, but I knew how hard it was to let walls down. "And I care about this nervous, gentle person in front of me now."

Ean was not the type to cry. He didn't swallow or blink or give any of the typical signs, but I sensed that if he'd ever been close to shedding a tear, it was right now.

"I'm so glad I get to see you be queen. Thank you, Your Majesty. For everything."

"Any time."

The song came to a close, and we bowed our heads to each other.

"Is it all right if I leave in the morning?" he asked. "I'd like to have some time with my family. To talk."

"Of course. Stay in touch."

He nodded and crossed the room, ready to begin his new life.

I'd done it. I'd made it through the day without doing anything humiliating, no one had protested, and I was still standing. It was over, and I could escape to the peace and quiet of my room.

And then when I was about to hit the side door, I saw Marid speaking in front of a camera.

He looked at me and lit up like a firework, waving me over to join in his interview. And while everything in me wanted to go and rest, his smile was so charming that I went to his side.

CHAPTER 23

"HERE SHE IS, THE LADY of the hour," he said, wrapping an arm around me as the interviewer giggled.

"Your Majesty, how are you feeling?" she asked, pointing the microphone at my face.

"Am I allowed to say tired?" I joked. "No, it's been an incredible day, and with so many distressing things happening in our country recently, I certainly hope today will lift everyone's spirits. And I'm very excited to get to work. Thanks to the wonderful young men in the Selection and friends, like Mr. Illéa here, I've gotten to know so much more about my people. I'm hoping we'll be able to find ways to hear and address needs much more efficiently."

"Can you give us any hints at what you're planning to do?" she asked eagerly.

"Well, I think our town hall meeting, which was completely

Marid's idea," I said, gesturing to him, "started off a bit rocky but was ultimately very informative. And Sir Woodwork actually had an interesting proposal recently about giving citizens a much easier way to petition the crown. I can't say too much about it at the moment, but it was incredibly inspired."

"Speaking of proposals," she said excitedly, "any news on that front?"

I laughed. "Let me get through my first week as queen and then I'll turn my focus back to dating."

"Fair enough. And what about you, sir? Any words of advice for our new queen?"

I turned to face Marid, who shrugged and ducked his head. "I just wish her all the luck with her reign, and finishing her Selection. The guy who wins her heart will be luckier than he knows."

Marid swallowed, seeming to have a hard time meeting the interviewer's eyes again.

She nodded heartily. "He certainly will." She turned to the camera and signed off, her attention no longer on us.

I took Marid's arm and swung him around, moving us out of earshot. "I don't want to be rude after all the kindness you've shown me, but behaving like that is inappropriate."

"Like what?" he asked.

"Like you and I might have been something if only the Selection hadn't happened. This is the third time I know of that you've said something like that, but I haven't even seen you in years. I am duty and honor bound to marry one of my candidates, so acting wounded when we've had absolutely nothing together is unacceptable. I must insist that you stop it at once."

"And why would I do that?" he said, his voice becoming slick.

"Excuse me?"

"If your family had been paying the slightest bit of attention to your people, you might have learned by now that when it comes to the public, I have an incredibly powerful voice. They treasure me. You should see the piles of fan mail I receive. Not everyone thinks the Schreave line is the valid one."

I froze, terrified that there was truth to what he was saying.

"You owe me a lot, Eadlyn. I've kept you looking good in papers and spoken well of you in interviews, and I saved that town hall meeting. I did that, not you."

"I could have—"

"No, you couldn't. And that's the problem. You can't do this job alone. It's nearly impossible, which is why you getting married is a wonderful idea. Only you're looking in the wrong place."

I was too stunned to speak.

"And, let's be honest: if any of those boys were that excited about you, wouldn't they be swarming around you this very second? From the outside looking in, they're all indifferent."

My shock turned to anguish. I looked around the room. He was right. None of the Elite seemed remotely aware of my presence.

"In the meantime, if you unite with me, the Illéa-Schreave

line will be completely secure. No one would dare question your right to rule if you were my wife."

The room swayed a little, and I fought to keep myself together as he went on. "And you can check the figures if you like, but as far as public opinion goes, my approval rating is twice what yours is. I could elevate you from tolerated to adored overnight."

"Marid," I said, hating that my voice sounded so weak. "This isn't possible."

"But it is. And either you can end this Selection on your own, or I can drop rumors about us to the point that no one takes it seriously anyway. By the time I'm done, you will look more heartless than they already think you are."

I straightened my back. "I will ruin you," I vowed.

"Try it. See how fast they turn on you." He kissed my cheek. "You have my number."

Marid walked away, casually shaking hands with those he passed as if he was already a member of the royal family. While all eyes seemed to follow him, I quietly ducked out of the room.

I was a fool. I'd thought that Hale cared about me, that Ean was here to support me, and I couldn't have been more mistaken. I'd been wrong to trust Burke and Jack and Baden. I'd been positive Marid was here to help me, and he'd only been trying to set himself on the throne. My instincts were wrong at every turn, and suddenly it seemed as though the people around me were nothing but fakes.

Was I mistaken about anyone else? Was I wrong to trust

Neena or Lady Brice? Was Kile not the friend I thought he was? Could I trust what I felt or thought about anyone?

I leaned against the wall, on the verge of tears. I was the queen. No one was as powerful as me. And yet I'd never felt more helpless.

Another figure came out of the doorway, and before I could duck farther out of sight, Erik's face came into view.

"Your Majesty, I'm sorry. I was just escaping the crowds. It was a little too much for me in there."

I didn't answer.

"Seems to have been a bit too much for you as well," he added cautiously.

I stared at the floor.

"Your Majesty?" He moved closer, whispering, "Can I help you?"

I stared into those wildly blue eyes and abandoned all the worries in my head. My heart said, *Run*. So I grabbed his hand and did just that.

I tore down the hallway, looking back once to make sure no one was following.

As I hoped, the Women's Room was empty. Leaving the lights off, I pulled us closer to the window, so at least I'd have the moon to help me see.

"At the risk of making an even bigger fool out of myself than I already have, can you please answer something for me? And you absolutely must be honest here. I give you permission to hurt my feelings. I *have* to know."

After a long moment he nodded, though his expression

told me he was terrified of what might come.

"Is there a chance that you feel for me the way I feel for you? If you've felt even a fraction of this riot that's been happening in my heart, I need to know."

Erik let out a breath, seeming stunned and sad at once. "Your Majesty, I—"

"No!" I said, ripping the crown off my head and flinging it across the room. "Not Majesty. Eadlyn. I'm just Eadlyn."

He smiled. "You are always just Eadlyn. And you are always the queen. You are everything to everyone. And infinitely more to me."

I placed a hand on his chest and could feel his heart pounding in time with mine. He suddenly seemed aware of how desperate I was and wordlessly cupped my cheek in his palm and leaned down to kiss me.

Every moment we'd ever had together danced through my head. His awkward stance the day we first met, and how I scolded him before the parade for biting his nails. The way he protected me when the fight broke out in the kitchen, and how my eyes flitted to him over and over when the boys were deep in prayer outside the hospital wing. And, most astonishingly, the moment in the Women's Room when Camille asked who filled my head, and how hard I fought to stop myself from saying his name out loud then and there.

All of it, every magical, forbidden second burned through me as we continued our dangerously treasonous kiss. When we finally broke apart, I was in tears, positive that Ahren leaving and the fear of losing my mother had been painless in comparison to this.

He shook his head, still holding on to me. "Of course the one time I let myself fall in love, it's with someone in another stratosphere."

I dug my fingers into his shirt, his vest, so angry that I couldn't hold on to it forever. "This will be the first time in my life I haven't been able to have something I truly wanted. It's so cruel that it happens to be you."

He swallowed. "It really is impossible then?"

My face fell. I didn't want to say the words. "I'm afraid so. In so many ways now. I can hardly grasp it all to explain, but everything just got much more complicated for me."

"You don't owe me an explanation. I already knew. I made the mistake of letting myself hope for a moment. That's all."

"I'm so sorry," I whispered, dropping my gaze. "If I thought I could cancel this whole thing, I would. But it would be seen as one more mistake on top of all the other selfish, stupid things I've done."

Using his other hand, he gently lifted my chin. "Please don't speak that way about the woman I love."

My smile was weak. "I've been so unfair to you. It was eating me alive, all the wondering, but maybe we would have been better off if we'd never known."

"No," he said, somehow able to find comfort in the middle of us being torn apart. "There is no shame in loving who you love, and there is great honor in doing what is right. It's a pity those two things don't overlap for us, but that makes this moment no less important to me."

"Or to me."

He held my hand so tenderly, still seeming shocked that he had the courage to do it at all.

"I should get back," he said. "I'd hate to cause a scandal."

I sighed. "You're right." And still I couldn't quite let go. I stood pressing myself to him. "I'm not engaged yet," I whispered. "Would you meet me tomorrow night?"

It was impossible not to see all the gears turning in his head. It was also easy to see the moment when he stopped thinking and nodded yes anyway.

"I'll get word to you. Leave now, and I'll make my way out in a few minutes."

Erik gave me one last hurried kiss and dashed back into the hall. Meanwhile, I retrieved my crown and walked over to the hidden panel behind the bookcase. I wanted to be sure no one would find me tonight.

There were no more rebels in Illéa, no threats like that to run away from. But there were still dozens of secret passages in the palace, and I knew every single one.

CHAPTER 24

"GOOD MORNING, YOUR MAJESTY," LADY Brice greeted me as I walked into the office. Typically, I'd been able to sleep in on Sundays, but there was no way I could spend my first day as queen in bed, especially not after the way things ended last night.

I sighed, both tired and thrilled. "I heard it a million times yesterday, but it still feels strange to answer to that title."

"You'll have decades to get used to it," she replied with a smile.

"Speaking of that, I need to speak with you about the Selection, and my reign, and an unexpected complication."

"Complication?"

"Can you tell me something? How popular is Marid?"

Lady Brice whistled. "He's made quite a name for himself over the last few years. He's frequently interviewed on the radio, and he's so handsome and comes from such a well-known family that he ends up in a lot of print media as well. Plenty of people listen when he speaks. Fortunate he decided to turn up when he did, huh?"

Before I could explain what had happened last night, I heard the door open behind me, and Josie burst into the room.

"Hey! Hope I'm not late!" she exclaimed.

I closed my eyes in frustration. I completely forgot she was supposed to start shadowing me today.

"Can I help you?" Lady Brice asked.

"Oh, I'm here to help *you*," she announced. "I'm shadowing Eadlyn today. Maybe longer, if this goes well."

"Miss Marlee suggested it during the family photo session yesterday," I said quickly.

Lady Brice nodded, and it was at this moment that Neena entered the office as well. Though I wasn't sure how comfortable I was sharing everything in front of Josie, it seemed I had no choice.

"Okay," I began slowly, "we have a problem. And his name is Marid Illéa."

"Really?" Neena asked. "He's seemed helpful so far."

"Yes, that was how he meant it to look. But, in truth, his goal has always been to take the crown." I swallowed, feeling stupid all over again. "Last night I called him out for encouraging the press to think that we were more than friends, and he made it clear that he was planning to pursue this angle until the public would demand that I marry him."

Lady Brice put her head in her hands. "I knew he could undermine this whole thing. I knew it. We should have squashed the rumors."

I shook my head. "This isn't your fault. You gave me the opportunity early on, and I didn't take it. I just never thought he'd try to worm his way into the palace as a permanent fixture."

"It's so sneaky," Lady Brice said, balling her hands into fists. "His parents threw rocks and stormed the palace. All he has to do is make a few properly timed speeches, and he's in without looking remotely aggressive."

"Exactly. And I'm . . . I'm scared. If he sways the people to believe he should be my prince consort, they'll come after the monarchy. They've been on the edge of revolt for a while, and now that I'm queen, there's nothing to stop the people who held out for my father's sake. But if we concede, and he's here . . . if he could lie that easily just to get near to me . . ."

"What would he do when he sees he doesn't need you anymore?" Lady Brice said somberly.

I'd already pictured a dozen different scenarios. He'd say I slipped down the stairs, or fell asleep in the bath, or that the Singer genes had gotten to my heart, too. I didn't want to think of Marid as purely evil, but I understood that he was out for power and had no regard for me.

It was possible I was being paranoid, I knew that. But after having missed so many things in the last few months, things that should have forced me to be careful, to speak up, to do something, now wasn't the time to assume things would be fine.

"Then we have to silence him. What do we do?" Neena asked.

"Why do you need to do anything?" Josie asked. We all turned, and her smile faded under the weight of our stares. "I mean, you're the queen. You could just kill him if you wanted. If he was being a traitor, right?"

"If he acts like a traitor, yes. But when it seems like he's in love with me and I decide to hang him, how does that make me look?"

She squinted, taking that in. "Awful."

"Worse than awful. And my approval is hanging on by a thread as it is. I can't have him killed. I don't even think I can publicly say I have no interest in him now, not without backlash."

"Then what?" Lady Brice asked.

"This doesn't leave the room. Does everyone understand?" I stared at Josie, hoping she understood the importance of secrecy. "First, we will ignore Marid. He's not allowed in the palace, and if he calls, no one speaks to him. He's completely shut out of my presence from here on out. We can't give the press so much as a whisper to draw from."

"Agreed," Lady Brice commented.

"Second, I've mapped out how the next few weeks will go in terms of the Selection. Ean is heading home this morning.

We spoke last night, and he's ready to go. Early next week Hale will be leaving as well."

Neena made a face. "I'm sad to see Hale go."

"Me, too. But this was a mutual agreement, so I assure you there are no hard feelings on either side."

"That makes it easier," she admitted. "But wait. Aren't you supposed to choose within four days once you get to a top three?"

"Yes. The only way to beat Marid at his game is to choose a husband as quickly as possible. And regardless of how deeply in love I may or may not be, it has to look as good as what my parents have. Better, if we can manage it." I took a deep breath. "So once Hale is gone, we'll wait a few days and then eliminate Fox. He's nice, but we don't have a real connection. That will leave Kile and Henri as the final two, and I intend to do a live broadcast in about two weeks to announce my fiancé."

"Two weeks!" Neena gasped. "Eadlyn!"

"I will need help with the perception of this," I went on. "I checked some recent poll numbers, and Hale and Kile have been front-runners for a while. I'll take care of making sure that Hale's decision to go is seen as necessary so the people will be satisfied with his departure, but we need something sensational about Henri. Like that he bakes for people in nursing homes or that his family is descended from Swendish nobility. Even if you have to stretch the truth, do it. Get him to the final two with everyone's approval."

No one spoke for a moment.

"Do you even love Kile?" Josie asked. For once her face had lost its ridiculously blank look, and I saw the deep, genuine concern in her eyes.

I thought of Erik. Of him promising me that it was worth it. Of how he'd treated me from the very start. Of how he'd kissed me.

Of how he'd be gone soon.

"I'd be happy with Kile."

Certainly leaders before me had made much bigger sacrifices, but Lady Brice, Neena, and Josie all looked as though I was marching into death.

"Are you going to help me or not?" I demanded.

"I'll see what I can find out about Henri," Lady Brice said. "I'd prefer to start with the absolute truth first."

"As would I. And I feel confident you'll be able to find something for him. He's such a sweetheart."

"He is," Neena agreed. "As is Kile. You could do much worse."

Yes, I thought. *But I could also do much better.*

"Do what you need to get everything in place for this. I'm going to spend the rest of the day working from my room. Josie?" She snapped to attention. "Are you coming back tomorrow, or was this enough for you?"

"It was more than enough," she said, swallowing.

"Not a word, you understand?"

She nodded, but I could hardly bear to look at her. She

seemed so sad for me, and of all people, I couldn't stand her pitying me. But when I looked at Neena and Lady Brice, their expressions were just as bad.

I pulled myself up as tall as I could and left the room, remembering that, no matter what, I was still queen.

CHAPTER 25

"WHAT IS THIS PLACE?" ERIK asked. I'd done my best to make it cozy, sneaking in with a basket full of candles and blankets midday, and another full of food when everyone left for dinner.

Erik said he was sick, I said I had work, and we met in an inconspicuous spot on the second floor. One of the easiest passages that led down to the massive safe room was by my mother's old bedroom, the one she'd had during her Selection. Sometimes she took pilgrimages there, like it was the calmest place for her to be in the palace.

"Back when the rebels were a deadly threat, the royal family used to escape down here," I told Erik as we made our way through the passage. "But this place hasn't been used in well over a decade, and now I think it may be the palace's best kept secret."

"In other words, no one's finding us," Erik responded with a smile.

"Not if we don't want them to."

He took a deep breath. "I've felt so guilty today, torn between how excited I was about your invitation and how guilty I feel since I'm not even a choice."

I nodded, pulling plates from the basket and setting them on top of the blankets. "I know. I've been cursing the Selection in ways I haven't since my parents first mentioned it. And then I take it all back, because if it had never happened . . ."

We shared a long look. I broke it with a sigh, continuing to set out our candlelit picnic.

"You know, my father wasn't supposed to marry my mother."

"You're kidding," he said, joining me.

"Apparently my grandfather had handpicked the girls who came to compete. He only threw in three Fives to appease the lower castes, and he hated Mom from the get-go. On top of that, I found out my parents used to argue all the time." I shrugged, still surprised by their rocky history. "I grew up thinking that they were a fairy tale, you know? It turns out they were just like anyone else. Somehow that makes it even more magical."

I let the words hang, thinking of everything I knew now.

"They slow dance when it rains. I have no idea why, but every time the sky turns gray, you'll find them together." I smiled. "I remember once Dad barged into the Women's Room, which is completely improper. You're supposed to be invited in. But it was raining, and he wasn't going to wait to sweep her away. And one time he dipped her in the hallway, and she just laughed and laughed. She was still wearing her hair down then, and I'll never forget how it looked like a waterfall of red. It's like no matter what happens, they can find themselves again there."

"I know what you mean." Erik eyed the bottle of red wine I'd snagged and grinned. "My parents find themselves over *omenalörtsy*."

I wrapped my arms around my knees, tucking my dress beneath me. "What's that?"

"It's like an apple doughnut. My mother made him a batch when they were dating, and it became their thing. When something good happens: *omenalörtsy*. When they're making up after a fight: *omenalörtsy*. When it seems like a particularly wonderful Friday: *omenalörtsy*."

"How did they meet?"

"This will sound strange, but through bolts and screws."

I squinted. "So . . . are they mechanics?"

"No," he replied with a chuckle. "My parents have known each other basically their entire lives. They grew up in the same small town in Swendway. When they were eleven, some guys at school were picking on my dad, throwing his schoolwork in the mud. My mom was even smaller than him at the time, but she went right up and yelled at them and pulled my dad away.

"He was embarrassed, but she was enraged. She forced him into an alliance, and that night they met each other on a back road, ran to each of the three bullies' houses, and stole the screws out of their bike wheels so they'd have to walk. For weeks after that, any time they saw that one of the bullies had replaced the screws, my mom and dad would go steal them. After a while the bullies gave up and walked."

"I like your mom," I said through bites of bread.

"Oh, you guys would get along great. She loves food and music and is on a constant hunt for a good reason to laugh. My dad, on the other hand— Well, if you think I'm shy, you should meet him. He's much more comfortable with books than people, and it can take him a while to warm up to strangers. Anyway, my parents grew up, and because they were very different people, they ran in different circles. Boy after boy came by for my mother, while my dad was spending weekends in the library.

"When my dad got older, he bought a bike. And one morning he woke up and found the screws for his wheels were missing."

"No!"

"Yes. And she did this until he wised up and started walking with her to school. And they've been walking together everywhere since."

"That is amazing."

He nodded. "They married young but waited awhile to start a family. They tell me not to take offense but that they weren't ready to share each other with anyone else, not even me."

I shook my head. "I really wish I could meet them."

"They'd have liked you. Dad might have spent most of the visit hiding in his room, but he'd have liked you all the same."

Erik uncorked the wine, and we shared fruit and bread and cheese. For a long time we didn't speak. The silence made everything feel bigger, better. There was no rush to fill the space, and after days and days of sound, the comfortable quiet with Erik was the most soothing thing in my world. It was like being alone without really being alone.

"I have to ask an embarrassing question," I admitted after a while.

"Oh, no." He took a deep breath. "All right, I'm ready."

"What's your full name?"

He nearly spit out his wine. "I thought I was going to have to confess some dark secret, and that's it?"

"I feel bad that I've kissed you and don't know your last name."

He nodded. "It's Eikko Petteri Koskinen."

"Eikko Pet . . . Petteri?"

"Koskinen."

"Koskinen."

"Perfect."

"Is it okay if I call you that? Eikko? I like your name."

He shrugged. "I only changed it because I thought it was too strange."

"No," I insisted. "It's not strange."

He looked down, toying with the blanket. "What about you? Full name?"

I sighed. "There was some debate over middle names, so it's Eadlyn Helena Margarete Schreave."

"That's a mouthful," he teased.

"It's pretentious, too. My name literally means 'princess shining pearl.'"

He tried to hide his smile. "Your parents named you Princess?"

"Yes. Yes, I am Queen Princess Schreave, thank you."

"I shouldn't laugh."

"And yet you do." I brushed the crumbs off my dress. "It makes me feel like I was predestined to become a brat."

He grabbed my hand, forcing me to look at him. "You are not a brat."

"The first time we really spoke, I corrected your manners."

He shrugged. "They needed correcting."

I smiled sadly. "I'm not sure why, but that makes me want to cry."

"Please don't. That was a good day for me."

I questioned him with my eyes, holding on to his hand as he continued. "When you got up onto the float and you were speaking with Henri? After you were done, you looked down to let me know everything was okay. You didn't have to do that. You were busy and in a rush, and you still acknowledged me. Even after knowing I was the type of person who bit my nails when I was nervous."

That made me want to cry even more. "Did it start then?"

"Pretty much. And I've chastised myself for it every day since. But, of course, I assumed no one would ever know, least of all you."

"I was a bit slower," I admitted. "I think it was when you pulled me from the kitchen. You weren't worried about what was happening, or how we might look running through a crowded room, or anything else in the world, it seemed. I was unsettled, and you brought me back to earth. So many people are in charge of keeping me in line, but no one seems to make me feel quite so normal as you."

He swallowed. "I'm sorry I won't be able to do that much longer."

"You have no idea how much I wish you could."

After a strained moment of silence, he cleared his throat. "Would you please be so kind . . . when this is over, would you please not contact me? I'm sure you could find me any time you wanted. But please don't. You have been a wonderful friend to me, and so have these men. I don't want to become the kind of man who betrays his friends."

"And I don't want to become the kind of woman who deceives her husband. When it's over, it's over."

"Thank you," he whispered.

"But nothing is over tonight," I reminded him.

He looked down, smiling a bit. "I know. I'm trying to decide if I have enough courage to ask you for another kiss."

I moved closer to him. "You can ask for one. Or two. Or twelve."

And he laughed before he toppled backward, the rush of our movement knocking over his glass of wine and sending the candle flames dancing.

CHAPTER 26

I GOT TO THE OFFICE a little later than I'd intended the next morning. I'd swept back my hair and dressed in a rush, but no matter how much time I spent on my face, I couldn't seem to wipe away my smile.

It was a delicious feeling, falling in love. I'd had so many luxuries in my life, and I thought I'd had a taste of this before, but I realized now it was merely a cheap imitation of something not meant to be imitated in the first place.

I reminded myself it would end, and I'd already made my peace with it. I knew I was going to choose Kile; I'd told Eikko as much.

Kile would make me happy, and I hoped I could do the same for him. I figured at some point, once Kile knew I was choosing him, I'd come clean to him about some of this. And I knew Kile well enough to know that he'd understand if I confessed to feeling confused about the process and that kissing Eikko wasn't something I planned, both of which were true. I didn't want it hanging over us. Any of us.

And a life side by side with Kile was not exactly a prison sentence. He was smart, passionate, funny, charming—a dozen things a husband ought to be. He would be beloved by the people—our people—and he would stand beside me and fight Marid. He was so charismatic, he might even render Marid useless.

And, deep in my heart, I hoped there was a chance that I could learn to love him, now that I knew what that really felt like.

For the time being I had a few precious days left with Eikko, and I intended to treasure each one.

Neena tapped on my desk, bringing my attention back to the present. "Are you okay? What are you thinking about?"

"Umm . . ."

To be honest, I was thinking about the sound of *Her Majesty Eadlyn Helena Margarete Schreave de Koskinen*, and how suddenly my mouthful of names seemed like a line of poetry. But then I looked into her eyes and saw they were tinged with red.

"About you," I said. "Are you all right?"

"I'm fine," she said in a tone that said *not really*. "It's just Mark. He's working such long hours, and now I have to work more, and it's getting harder to keep in touch. You know, same old. Distance isn't a big deal until it is."

I took her hands. "Neena, the last thing I want to do is

cost you the person you love. You're a brilliant girl; you could work anywhere—"

"Are you firing me?" she whispered, looking like she might cry.

"Of course not! The thought of you leaving breaks my heart. If you can have friend soul mates, you're mine, and I don't want you going anywhere." She laughed through her glassy eyes. "I just can't bear to watch you lose something that matters so much to you."

"I get that. Do you have any idea how hard it is for me to sit back and look at your life right now?"

I sighed. "My life is a different thing entirely. And, like you said, I could do worse."

"Eadlyn, please rethink this. There must be a better way to stop Marid."

"If there is, I don't have the time to wait for it. If I don't secure my place now, I'll either have a reign filled with people trying to usurp me and failing, or people trying and succeeding. Those options aren't acceptable. This matters to me. I can't compromise."

She nodded. "Well, neither can I. And I couldn't leave you like that."

I took her hand, grateful, as always, for her presence in my life.

"Let me know if you change your mind," I insisted. "If you need to leave, I could—"

I was stunned into silence by the sight of Josie coming into the office balancing a tray in her hands. She set a cup of coffee in front of Neena and one in front of me before she spoke.

"Everyone said you took your coffee with two sugars, but if it's wrong I can go back."

"No, no," I said, still slightly confused. "That's right."

"Okay. And I was walking by the mailroom and they had these, so I figured I could get them to you." She placed a handful of letters in the wooden in-box on my desk.

"Thank you."

She nodded. "Also, I saw your mother this morning. She's doing very well. I haven't seen any of the boys."

"Good luck hunting them down," I said with a smile. "Thank you, Josie."

"It's the least I could do." She shrugged. "I'm not busy, if you need another set of hands."

"Neena?"

I turned, and saw she was still taking in this change. "How's your penmanship?" she finally asked.

"Excellent," Josie replied, beaming.

"All right, then." And just like that, I got an unexpected addition to the office.

Fox was quiet as we walked the palace halls. It wasn't the most exciting of dates, but the constant cloud of worry hanging over my head had sapped any creativity I had. Still, as the photographer checked the images on the back of his camera, he seemed pleased.

"It's kind of sad that we can't go out to a restaurant or do something fun like . . . Do you bowl?" Fox asked.

"No," I answered with a laugh. "Putting on shoes that a thousand other people have worn and putting my fingers into holes with goodness knows how many germs in there?" I stuck out my tongue. "Not my thing."

He smiled. "But it's so fun! How can you even think about germs?"

"Osten once asked to go bowling for his birthday. We rented an entire bowling alley for the afternoon. After I realized you were supposed to wear used shoes, I couldn't get over it. No matter how much disinfectant they sprayed in there, I wasn't up for that. Everyone played, even Mom, but I watched."

"That's sad. Are you afraid of germs?" His tone was almost mocking.

I let the snub go. "No. It's just incredibly unappealing."

"Well, that settles it," he said.

"Settles what?"

"If you marry me, the first order of business is putting in our own personal bowling alley."

I laughed.

"I'm not kidding. Maybe we could do away with the studio and put it there."

"No more *Reports*?" I asked joyfully. "Okay, that might be a tipping point for me. I'm on board."

"You could design your own shoes!"

"Ooooh!" I could already imagine taking those weird shoes and making them worthy of royalty. That would be a fun project. "That's one thing I really like about you, Fox. You're good at lightening the mood."

"I think we're good, Your Majesty," the photographer said, retreating. "Thank you."

"Thank you," I called. "Sorry about that. With things getting to the end, people really want a peek into the final four."

"Oh, I don't mind," he said. "I feel lucky, getting this far, getting to be with you."

I rubbed my thumb across his hand. "Thanks, Fox. I know I've been busy."

"Do I look upset? I'm on the first date with you as queen. How incredible is that?"

I hadn't even considered how that might be taken. I'd been hoping to hint that he might be leaving soon. Now I felt trapped.

"I've been so rude. How are you doing? How's your family?"

"Dad's all right. He's been bragging to everyone who'll stop and listen. 'You saw Fox was in the final four, right? That's my boy.'" He shook his head. "I guess he hasn't had much to celebrate for a while, so even though I kind of want to tell him to calm down, I can't. At least I don't have to watch it firsthand."

I giggled. "I know what you mean. My dad's into photography, and he likes to document every little thing. For some reason it can be way more embarrassing when he's there than a journalist, even when they're doing the exact same thing."

"It's your dad. It's personal."

"Yeah."

We fell silent, and the palace felt empty. For a moment I missed the crowding mass of boys who'd stormed into my life barely two months ago. I wondered if I would keep thinking about them after this was all over.

"Anyway, he's doing well, all things considered," Fox said, filling the space. "He's really proud, but he keeps asking me questions that I'm never quite sure how to answer."

"What do you mean?"

I watched Fox's expression shift from determination to embarrassment.

"He keeps asking me if I love you. Or if you love me. I've told him that I can't go walking into your office and demanding a declaration of love." He grinned, showing he understood how unreasonable the request was. "I would never ask you to tell me your feelings. I'm not sure that's fair. But I thought you should know that I . . . I . . ."

"Don't say it."

"Why not? I felt it for a while now, and I've wanted to tell you."

"I'm not ready to hear it." I backed away, my heart pounding in my ears. This was too fast, too sudden. I'd hardly gotten to speak to him recently, and now this?

"Eadlyn. I want you to at least know how I feel. You're going to have to pick someone soon, so wouldn't it be wise for you to have this information?"

I turned to him and squared my shoulders. If I could face

reporters and dignitaries, I could face a boy. "Tell me everything, Fox."

His smile was tiny but sincere. "I think I've been a goner for you from the night you let me stay. You were so kind to me in the middle of the worst night of my life, and I'm desperate for you to meet my family. I want to see you on the beach in Clermont; I want you to spend an evening around the table with us. In a million ways, I think you'd fit right in with the Wesleys."

He paused, shaking his head like he couldn't believe he'd said that.

"I want to help you. I want to be there for you in any way I can. And I'd like to think that you could be there for me. I don't know how much longer I have with my dad. I'd like him to know I've chosen a path before he dies."

I closed my eyes, feeling overwhelmed with guilt. It wasn't that long ago my mother was on what I thought was her deathbed. I understood that wish.

"But that doesn't mean I can make it come true," I mumbled.

"What?"

"Nothing," I answered, shaking my head clear. "Fox, these are beautiful sentiments. And I admire your honesty, but I'm not ready to make any promises."

"I'm not asking you to." He came closer, taking my hand. "I just needed you to know how I felt."

"And now, as you said, I'll take all this into consideration as I'm making my choice. Which will be soon."

He rubbed his finger across my hand, a gesture that felt less comforting than it should have.

"I'm serious about you, Eadlyn. Don't doubt it."

"Oh, I don't," I whispered. "Not in the slightest."

CHAPTER 27

"I DON'T UNDERSTAND," NEENA CONFESSED the next morning as I recounted the date to her. "Isn't him confessing his devotion a good thing? Like, maybe he could be one of the top two instead?"

Everyone else was still at breakfast, so the office was empty. As the sun beamed through the windows, we sat together on a couch, legs curled beneath us, as if this was the morning after a slumber party.

"I don't think so. Something about it felt so forced. Not that he didn't actually feel those things, but it was like he orchestrated a moment so I would have to hear it." I rested my head on my hand, the lines repeating in my head. "And then I felt guilty. He talked about his dad and said I'd make a good Wesley and . . . it was all just off somehow."

My free hand picked at the hem of my skirt as if my fingers

could undo my tangled thoughts. "I think what it was," I began, "is that he said he'd felt this way since the night of the kitchen fight, but we haven't really had much interaction since then, at least not one-on-one. So for him to have this growing, deep, serious attraction to me . . . where does it stem from?"

Neena nodded. "It's like he's in love with someone he thinks you are, not who you really are."

My whole body wilted in relief. "That's it. That's exactly what this feels like."

"So send him home?"

I shook my head. "No, I promised Hale he could leave next. He's ready, and I don't want to disappoint him, not after everything he's done for me."

"Good morning, Your Majesty. Hi, Neena." Lady Brice walked in, holding a muffin in her hand. "Your Majesty, I have some documents from your brother for you to review. It appears France wants to renegotiate their trade deal. I think this will be the easiest one in years."

"Aww, what a handy little thing, that Ahren." I was sure this was more Camille's doing than his, but I knew his presence was helpful.

"He sure is. I also have three contracts for you to review from New Asia; they're waiting on your desk. And the producer of the *Report* would like to film an interview with you this afternoon, something about transition pieces, I don't know."

"Oh, so, a nice, easy day?" I joked.

"As always!"

"Lady Brice, did you help Dad this much?"

She laughed. "Only for a short time. Once you grew up, he wanted you to take on a bigger role. And as soon as you feel you're on your feet, I'll happily step back, or maybe retire."

I scrambled off the couch and grabbed her by the shoulders. "No. Not ever. You will live and die in this office!"

"As you wish, my queen."

"Your Majesty! Your Majesty!" someone yelled.

"Josie?" I called, watching as she ran in. "What's the matter?"

"I was watching TV. Marid." She was gulping in breaths.

"What about Marid?"

She swallowed. "He was seen shopping for engagement rings. It's all over the news."

All the advisers flooded into the parlor as we watched everything unfold. Very quickly, the many people I didn't trust with my secrets were made all too aware of what Marid had been plotting and just how close he was coming to the crown.

"He's got the look of a king, doesn't he?" one newscaster said.

"Of course he does! He's descended from one!" her cohort replied.

"Really, wouldn't that be so romantic?"

"It would. Oh, it so would, but she is in the middle of a Selection."

The newscaster brushed her hand across the air. "Who cares? Let them go. None of them has the charm of Marid Illéa, not by a long shot."

I flipped channels.

"According to the jeweler, Mr. Illéa was looking at some rather expensive pieces, which would only be fitting if he is indeed planning to propose to the queen."

"This is yet another unlikely event in a series of unprecedented moves surrounding the royal family. First, we have a Selection led by a princess instead of a prince. Second, we have a young woman ascending well before she's been either fully trained or her father has passed. And now we have an outside suitor trying to steal the queen's heart before one of the Elite has a chance. It is absolutely fascinating."

I flipped channels again.

"Kathy here was on hand when the young Mr. Illéa came in. Can you tell us what you saw?"

"Well, he seemed a little bashful at first, as if he wasn't ready to admit why he was here. But after about fifteen minutes of him lingering along the case, it was pretty obvious what he was looking for."

"And did he seem drawn to anything in particular?"

"He had me pull out at least a dozen different rings, and when nothing was quite what he was looking for, I told him we could design a piece for him if he liked, and he lit up. I'm hoping he comes back soon."

"So would you choose Marid over, say, Sir Hale or Sir Kile?"

"Oh, goodness! I really can't say. All I know is, Queen Eadlyn is a very lucky woman to have so many eligible men fawning all over her."

I couldn't take it anymore. I turned off the TV and fell with a huff onto the couch.

"I should have known," I said. "Silence seemed smart, but now he's made this huge."

Mr. Rasmus grunted. "We need a plan."

"We have a plan," I snapped. "Is there anything we really could have done besides marrying me off faster?"

General Leger stood with his back against a bookshelf, still staring at the blank screen. "We could kill him."

I sighed. "I really don't want that to be my go-to move."

Sir Andrews was angry, too, but for all the wrong reasons. "You shouldn't have provoked him."

"I've done nothing," I shot back.

"You were actively ignoring him."

"Calm down, Andrews." Lady Brice paced behind the couch, enraged. As I watched her, I caught Josie standing in a corner. She must have missed her opportunity to escape and was now trapped, looking afraid of the loud voices and anger that surrounded her. "We have to shut him up, once and for all."

"The only way to do that is to get Eadlyn engaged," Sir Andrews stated.

"Yes, we're aware," Lady Brice agreed in a tired tone. "But she shouldn't be rushed into this. How can she have anything close to a successful marriage if she forces it?"

"It's her duty to make it successful!"

"Duty? She's a person," Lady Brice argued. "She's agreed to do this, and there's no reason—"

"She has never been just a person!" Andrews reminded her. "From the second she was born, she's been a commodity, and we need to—"

General Leger was moving toward Andrews. "Say that again. I'm not afraid to make death *my* go-to move."

"Are you threatening me, you little—"

"Stop," I breathed. And it was amazing. With the quietest of commands, the entire room came to a standstill.

I'd known it was coming for me. And I really had come to terms with it. Marid had shown how much influence he truly had, and I had to fight him off. I couldn't help worrying that even marriage wouldn't keep the people on my side, but it was all I had left. "Lady Brice, if you would, please, bring Fox to the office. It's time we said our good-byes."

"Are you sure, Your Majesty? Once you narrow it down to three—"

"I'm not narrowing it down to three." I swallowed. "Please send Hale soon after. I'll be making my final choice this evening, and we will do a live broadcast tomorrow night instead of a *Report*. No doubt, after this week, everyone will be watching."

"Absolutely, Your Majesty."

"There, Sir Andrews. You have your progress. My official engagement announcement will come from the palace tomorrow afternoon."

"Are you sure we ought to wait that long? If Marid—"

"If Marid pulls another stupid stunt, it will be shot down in less than twenty-four hours. That is good enough for me, sir, so it is certainly good enough for you."

I stood. It was done.

I was certain something would give me away, convinced that everyone in the room would see that a part of me had lost oxygen and was suffocating then and there. In my head, I watched Eikko pack his suitcase and disappear from my life forever. It was a new kind of pain, pressed into this doomed heart of mine.

CHAPTER 28

EVERYONE LEFT IN A HUFF for lunch, and I stayed in the parlor, craving solitude. In truth, I craved Eikko, but there was no way I could get to him without raising suspicion. Gritting my teeth, I turned the TV back on. I muted it, watching the images of Marid play across the screen.

Maybe the people were right. Maybe I should step down now. If we trained Kaden for the crown, that might save everything. It would be humiliating for me to abdicate after less than a week, but it might at least keep the rest of my family from being shamed.

"Your Majesty?" Josie snuck up on me. "Can I get you anything? Some food? Coffee?"

"No, Josie. I've lost my appetite."

"I don't blame you," she said with a tiny smile.

"I want to thank you for coming to warn me today. I

know it doesn't seem like much, but those extra five minutes helped me brace myself. It would have been a thousand times worse if Sir Andrews had found out first."

She widened her eyes. "He's horrible. Do they yell like that all the time?"

I nodded. "Not Lady Brice or General Leger. But the others were like that with Dad, too. It's as if they think the only way to make you understand how adamant they are is to scream about it."

We were quiet for a minute, watching Marid's handsome face on the screen. He certainly had his wave down.

"I'm so sorry, Eadlyn," Josie whispered, drawing my focus back to her. "For everything, and for how I've been, and for what you're dealing with now."

"You had no idea, did you?" I asked, my tone gentle.

Embarrassed, she shook her head. "I thought everyone did the work for you, and you just said yes or no."

"That it was all parties and money and power?"

"Yeah." She let out an almost laugh. "I can't believe I spent my whole life wanting to be a princess only to see I could never, ever handle it."

I shifted on the couch, finally putting to voice a thing I'd been almost positive about from the very beginning.

"Is that why you put Kile's name in? So you could be a princess?"

She blushed fiercely. "I didn't think he'd actually get drawn. And if he did, I didn't think there was any way you'd choose him. When I saw that kiss on the front page of the newspapers, I was so excited. I started designing tiaras in my notebooks."

"And now?"

"I'd still like to have one of my very own, but I know I haven't earned it." She smiled slowly. "And I realize that even if he wins, I wouldn't exactly be a princess, but it still feels like a big deal. I look at your aunt May, and how glamorous she is, traveling around the world and meeting all these people and looking like a runway model."

"I can see the appeal," I agreed. "Mom's siblings definitely got a better deal than she did in certain ways."

As I thought of my aunt and uncles, a wonderful idea struck me, and I was thrilled that at least one good thing might come from this day.

Josie played with the hem of her dress. "Yeah, it looks fun. But I was way too obsessed with it. I'm sorry I gave you such a hard time."

"So am I. It was hard growing up with someone who wanted to be me without doing any of the work."

"And it was hard for me growing up in your shadow." She seemed sad, unsure of herself now.

"You know, Josie, it isn't too late to fall in love with something else. You happen to have an excellent resource in me, and I'd like to help you find the right path. So long as that path is far away from my tiaras."

She giggled. "I have no idea where to start."

"Well, you've proven these last few days how helpful you can be. What if we put you on the payroll, as an office intern? Whatever you're going to do, you'll need your own money for it."

"Really?" she gasped.

"Really."

Josie flung herself across the room, colliding with me in a hug. For the first time, I didn't mind her being so close.

"Thank you."

"You're welcome. I've got to do the good I can while I'm here."

She pulled back. "I swear, if you step down, I'll never forgive you."

I hadn't meant to give that much away in a sentence.

"I realize that doesn't mean much, but still. Don't do it. You can't."

I shook my head. "I won't. I promise. As tempting as it is, I'm too proud to do it."

Dear Uncle Gerad,
This letter is long overdue. How are you? How's work? How's . . .

Okay, I need a favor. My lady-in-waiting's boyfriend is also a talented scientist. I'm not completely sure if his field and yours are similar, but I thought you might at least have a connection that could get him work in Angeles. It would mean the world to her if he was closer,

and it would mean the world to me if she was happier.
Do you think you could help?

Friendly reminder, I'm your queen.

Thanks bunches! Love you lots! Visit soon!

Eadlyn

CHAPTER 29

FOX UNDERSTOOD WHAT BEING SUMMONED to my office meant. So he refused to come and instead sent his good-byes through Neena, who arranged for him to stay at a hotel until he could get a flight to Clermont the following morning.

I felt low, sneaky somehow, like I'd gotten off too easy. I'd been prepared for a battle. I got a retreat.

But Hale walked through the doorway all smiles, dressed to the nines and ready to leave like a gentleman. His arms were open as he crossed the office, and I fell into them, trusting him to a fault.

"I'm going to miss you so much," he whispered into my ear.

"Me, too. But you know how to get ahold of me if you need to, right?"

He nodded. "Neena gave me some information along with my flight details."

"Good. Because I'm probably going to need to speak with you soon."

"Oh?" he asked, stepping back and straightening his suit coat.

"Of course. *Someone* has to design my wedding dress."

Hale stood there, the smile wiped instantly from his face as if he thought this was some twisted joke.

"Eadlyn . . . do you mean that?"

I held him by the shoulders. "You shielded me when the public threw food. You befriended me before I was willing to accept it. Even now you've protected me, far past anything I've deserved. The least I can do is be your first client. I'll be watching your skyrocketing career with interest, sir."

His eyes glistened with tears, but he managed to keep himself together.

"I'm kind of scared to leave," he confessed. "So much is going to change once I'm outside of these walls."

I nodded. "But that doesn't mean it's going to all be bad."

He laughed. "When did you become such an optimist?"

"It comes and goes."

"As do most things," he said with a sigh.

"As do most things," I agreed. I hugged him one last time. "Have a safe flight, and start designing as soon as you get home."

"Are you kidding? I'll be designing in the car!"

Hale kissed my cheek and winked. "Bye, Eadlyn."

"Bye."

With Hale gone, everything spiraled into a laser focus. This was the end. There were two suitors left, and one blue-eyed soul mate. I wasn't sure who to speak to first. After some thought, I realized Eikko knew what was coming. He wouldn't be surprised by my announcement. But Henri would, and I expected he was going to take it hard. I would see Kile first, and that would leave me plenty of time to talk this out calmly with Henri through the painful use of his positively wonderful translator.

I was trembling when I knocked on Kile's door. I hadn't prepared a speech or anything. And while I assumed he'd say yes, I really had no idea. What if he'd suddenly decided that I wasn't worth all the work?

His butler answered the door and bowed deeply. "Your Majesty."

"I need to speak with Sir Kile, please."

"I'm sorry, miss, he's not here. He mentioned getting something from his old room."

"Oh. Well, I know where that is. Thank you."

I made my way up to the third floor, following the path I'd taken the night he'd agreed to kiss me in the hallway. What a strange turn our lives had taken.

Kile's door was slightly open, and I could see him tinkering away in the corner of his room. He'd flung his suit jacket and tie on the bed and was sanding a small piece of wood, presumably preparing to attach it to the structure beside it.

"Can I come in?"

He whipped his head up, and a few strands of hair fell into his face. It was getting long again. It didn't look as bad as I remembered.

"Hey there," he said, shaking the mess off his hands and coming to greet me. "I was hoping I'd get to see you today."

"Oh, yeah?"

He put an arm around my waist and pulled me to the back of the room. "I was watching some TV this morning, and I kept seeing all this stuff about Marid."

I rolled my eyes. "I know. He's a bit of a problem right now."

He swept some dust off a chair, and I sat across from him, looking at his little creations. Detailed sketches in blue and black ink, piles of books with papers sticking out, and his miniature buildings scattered around like a tiny town. He'd made a world up here.

"Can he really propose?" He sounded nervous, like he feared Marid might take me instead of the country.

"He can, I suppose, but I won't say yes." I sighed. "Turns out Marid is not the ally I thought he was. He's been threatening to sway public opinion, and at first I wasn't sure he could do it. Then the way he got himself into everyone's house today . . . it's brilliant, really. Just like Lady Brice said, it's an instant, battle-free invasion."

"Invasion? Like what? Is he suddenly vying for the crown?"

I ran my fingers over the lines of one of Kile's drawings.

"I don't think it's sudden. I think he and his family have been looking to make a move for quite a while. The inept young queen was a perfect opportunity.

"Now he wants to be my consort and use my name to make his plans happen. My only hope is to get engaged before he can try to propose, because I'm sure the press will just gobble it up if I reject him."

"So let's do it."

"Do what?"

"Get married. Eadlyn, I'd marry you tonight. Between the two of us and our families, there's no way he'd survive. People have been pulling for us from the start. Marry me, Eadlyn."

I looked into the sweet and worried face of Kile Wood-work, and for a minute I really thought I could. I'd told myself it would all be easy, to walk down an aisle and find him at the end. He'd always make me laugh. And after the last two months of being on the same side, I knew, without question, that he would support me for life.

"I will confess, I came here just now to make that very proposal. But . . . I can't."

"Why? Is it because I didn't get down on one knee?" He dropped instantly, gripping my hands. "Or wait, is it because you're supposed to ask?"

I got down on the floor with him. "No. It's not because of any of that."

His face fell. "You don't love me."

I shook my head, laughing. "No, it's not that either. In

fact, I might love you a little too much. Maybe not entirely romantically, but I definitely love you."

"Then why?"

"Because of this," I said, motioning to the work around me. "Kile, I'll never be able to tell you how much it means to me that you would take me for life just to save me from one person. Considering what a pain I've been, that's a miracle."

He chuckled, still holding my hands.

"But all you have ever wanted was to get away from these walls. All you want to do is build. I think that's a beautiful thing. So many people in the world want to tear things apart. How wonderful is it that you'd do the opposite?"

"But I'd give it up. I wouldn't mind."

"*I* would. I would mind. And eventually, when the scary side of my life dies down, you would, too. You'd die a little from the ache for it. You'd resent me." Tears pooled in my eyes. "I can't live in a world where you don't like me."

"I'll stay, Eady. I'm telling you, I want to."

"I can't."

"You can. You just said that you needed to. Who could do this better than me?"

Hot tears streamed down my face. "Please, don't make me force this on you."

"You can't make me leave, Eadlyn."

I ripped my hands from his and shot to my feet, wiping my face. I looked down on Kile, my sweet, sacrificing friend, and steadied myself.

"Kile Woodwork, you are hereby banished from the

palace for the term of one year."

"What?" he stood, balling his fists.

"As compensation for losing your home, and for services rendered to the royal family, you will have an apartment fully paid for in Bonita."

"Bonita? That's on the other side of the country!"

"In addition, funds and materials will be allotted to you to begin a housing project for the homeless in the province's capital city."

His face softened. "What?"

"If you find the funds or materials insufficient, you may write the palace and request more, and I will have them sent to you as quickly as possible."

"Eadlyn . . ."

"You will always be my family, Kile, but I won't make you my husband. I can't do that to you."

His voice was tender. "But you will make *someone* your husband. You need to now."

"It will be Henri. Fox left a few hours ago, and Hale just got into a car."

He was completely floored. "This is really the end, isn't it?"

"And I was prepared to be with you for the rest of my life. In a way, I guess I still can. But I'd hate myself if I kept you here. It'd be heartless."

"What about Henri? Will you be happy with him?"

I swallowed. "He does worship the very ground I walk on."

Kile nodded, allowing that. "I suppose you could do worse than absolute devotion."

I smiled. "Thank you. You have kept me sane through so much of this, but I can't take away the one thing you really care about."

He nodded. "I understand."

I walked toward him, and he folded me into an embrace, holding me so close it almost hurt.

His voice sounded tight when he finally spoke. "If there's anything I can ever do for you, tell me."

I wept into his shirt. "I will. And I'll do anything you ask."

"Except marry me."

I pulled back, happy to see him smile. "Except marry you." I let go, lacing my fingers together. "I'm going to make the official announcement tomorrow. I need you to stay until then so the press doesn't get wind of what's going on. After that, I don't want to see your face for a year. You hear me, Woodwork?"

"I get a pass for the wedding, right?"

"Well, of course, for the wedding."

"And Christmas?"

"Obviously."

He considered. "What about your birthday?"

"Well, Ahren did say he'd come back, so it'll probably be a marvelous party."

He nodded. "Okay then. A year except for those three days."

"Perfect. And in the meantime, you'll just be doing the

thing you were born to do," I said with a shrug, as if this was all nothing.

He shook his head. "I'm going to build something. I'm really going to build something."

"And you will change lives because of it."

"Thank you, Your Majesty."

"You're welcome." I kissed his cheek and ran out of the door before I changed my mind. "I'll see you in the studio tomorrow. I'll send details once I have them."

In the hallway, I held my hand to my stomach and took a deep breath. I'd made a choice. So why did I suddenly feel out of control?

I hurried back to the office, glad to see that everyone was on the move, making tomorrow come together as smoothly as possible. Everyone it seemed, except for me.

"Lady Brice, can you please get Erik for me? I need to speak with him about the specifics of tomorrow."

"Consider it done."

CHAPTER 30

I PACED THE OFFICE'S SIDE parlor, waiting for him to come. Every second, the mass in my throat grew bigger, threatening to trap all the words I had to say beneath it.

"Your Majesty?" he said quietly, and even though there were people swarming around, he didn't think twice about smiling at me like I was his sun and stars.

"I need to speak with you about tomorrow. Would you close the doors, please?" I tried to keep my voice even, but his expression showed he knew I was holding back. And that made the attempt at diminishing how important this was that much harder.

"Are you all right?" he whispered, even though we were alone.

I exhaled, trying to keep calm. "Not quite."

"According to the news, you have an unexpected suitor," he said plainly.

I nodded.

"How long has this been a problem?"

"Longer than I knew."

"I imagine this has caused you undue stress."

"It's done so much more than that." I swallowed. "Because of this issue, I am forced to announce my engagement tomorrow."

"Oh." The tiny word held a world of shock.

"And due to Kile having other pursuits that I couldn't ignore, I will be proposing to Henri. Today."

At that he couldn't muster a word at all.

I reached for his hand, and he gave it to me. He didn't even look angry, which would have been fair since I'd backed out of nearly every promise I'd made. He was, quite simply, only sad. A feeling I identified with all too well.

"I'm sure you understand that I will have to leave after tomorrow," he said quietly.

"I'll have Neena find another translator. You shouldn't be forced to replace yourself." My breathing hitched, and the tears came. "I'm planning on going within the hour to see him. Do you think . . . could you please not be in the room?"

He nodded. "If you had asked me to stay, it might be the first time I tried to refuse you."

We stood there, quietly holding hands. Maybe if we were still, nothing could change.

"I'd prepared myself," he said. "I understood what was coming and still—"

The pain of standing there watching Eikko's lip tremble was acute.

I fell into him. "Eikko, I need you to hear it. Just once, I need you to know it without doubt. I love you. And if I was free, if I was my own person, I'd escape with you now. But Marid would use my absence as a reason to take the throne, and my people." I shook my head. "I can't. . . ."

He took my face in his hands, making me look into his eyes. Though they brimmed with tears, they were as beautifully clear as ever. "What a privilege it is to come in second place to your people. What a queen you've become, that you can't bear to part yourself from them."

I pulled him to me, kissing him as if our lives depended on it. Maybe it wasn't the prettiest kiss, with moisture under our noses and mascara on my cheeks, but it was the encapsulation of all the other ones we'd never get to have.

Kile was right. It was the last kisses that mattered.

I stepped back, wiping my face. I really wanted to be a lady in this moment. I reached down, slipping his great-great-grandmother's ring off my finger.

"Don't be silly."

"It's an heirloom, Eikko."

He wrapped his hand around mine. "The day I gave it to you, I had no intention of taking it back. I couldn't give it to anyone else."

I smiled sadly and put it back in place. "Well, then." I

reached down and pulled my signet ring off instead.

"Eadlyn, that is for royalty."

"And you would have been an excellent prince. For the rest of your life, you'll have proof."

We stared down at our rings. They weren't on our left hands, but it was as close as we'd get. A part of my heart would always be locked away for Eikko.

"I have to go," he said. "He should be in his room."

I nodded.

Eikko gave me a faint kiss on my cheek and whispered in my ear, "I love you. I hope you have a beautiful life."

And then, as if he couldn't take another second, he slipped back out through the office, sliding the door closed behind him.

I sat down, gripping the arm of the couch. I felt positively sick. Like I might faint. Or vomit. I ran to the door that led straight to the hallway, dashing to my room as quickly as I could.

"My lady?" Eloise asked as I bolted past her and into the bathroom, heaving up everything I'd eaten today.

Between bursts of sickness I wailed, furious and broken and just so tired.

"Get it all out," Eloise whispered, coming over with a damp cloth. "I've got you."

She knelt behind me and wrapped her arms around my stomach. The pressure was surprisingly soothing.

"I can't imagine what it's like to be you. Everyone having an opinion, everyone having a request. But when you're here, you scream and you cry all you want, okay? We'll get you through it."

I sobbed, turning myself in to her chest. She didn't even say a word, just held me as I let everything flood out of my system.

"Thank you," I said when my breathing had slowed.

"Any time. Now, do you need to get back to work?"

"I have to go propose to Henri."

If she was surprised, she didn't show it. "First things first. Let's wash your face."

And with that I began the slow process of preparing myself for the first step of the rest of my life.

CHAPTER 31

ELOISE HELPED ME PULL MYSELF together, and I looked nothing short of magnificent when I walked down to Henri's room. Just as I'd done when I thought I'd end up with Kile, I reminded myself that this wasn't a bad choice. Henri would be devoted and kind, and while our means of communication might be unconventional for a while, it didn't mean that our life together wouldn't be a happy one.

His butler answered the door and kindly ushered me in. Henri was at his table with books opened and a pitcher of tea at his disposal. He stood when he saw me, bowing in a way that could only be described as joyful.

"Hello today!"

I giggled, walking over with the wide wooden box in my arms. "Hello, Henri." I set it down on his table and hugged him, and he brightened at my affection. "What's all this?"

I touched his books, taking in the pages. Of course, even if he had no help, he was studying his English. He grabbed at a notebook and held it up, pointing.

"I write for you. I can read, yes?"

"Oh, yes, please."

"Okay, okay." He took a deep breath and smiled as he held up his papers. "'Dear Eadlyn. I know I cannot be saying, but I am thinking of you each days. My words are no good yet, but my heart,'" he said, touching his chest, "'feels what I cannot saying. Even in Finnish, I would say them bad.'"

He laughed at himself and shrugged, and I smiled.

"'You have beautiful, talent, smartness, and are nice. I hope to showing you how good I think of you. Also, more kissing.'"

I couldn't not laugh, and he was so happy to see me in good spirits, he looked like he might burst from it.

"Still working," he said, sitting the notebook down. "Um, I getting Erik?"

"No," I said. "Just you."

He looked nervous at trying to communicate with me on his own. But even this was better than we'd ever done before. He nodded, rubbing his hands together to get out some of his nervous energy.

"Henri, you like me, yes?"

He nodded. "Yes. Like you."

"I like you, too."

He smiled. "Good!"

And again I found myself laughing. *See, Eadlyn, this would be fine.*

"Henri . . . Henri, would you marry me?"

He squinted for a moment before his eyes widened in surprise.

"I marry you?"

"Yes, if you would like to."

He stepped back, smiling as always, but there was something in his expression I couldn't name. Disbelief? Doubt? But after a flicker of a second, it disappeared.

"Wait, wait." He dropped to his knees, clutching both of my hands. "You will marry me?"

"Yes."

He laughed and went to kissing my hands over and over, finally stopping and staring at them for a while, like he couldn't believe he was going to hold them for the rest of his life.

"Come here," I said, urging him to stand.

He embraced me, holding me tight. And as sweet as all this was, I was fighting the urge to cry again.

"You have to give me a ring," I said, and opened the box on the table, taking in Henri's audible gasp.

Set in the blue velvet were twenty-five different engagement rings, ranging in size and color but all befitting a queen.

He stared at them a second before turning to me. "I pick for you?"

"Yes."

He made a face, a little overwhelmed with his options.

Henri ran his finger over the dreamy combinations of garnet and amethyst and lingered over the diamonds so flat and wide, you could go ice-skating on them. But then he found a large pearl, set in a blushing rose gold and surrounded by a string of diamonds. He held it up to his face and nodded.

"For you."

I held out my left hand, and he slipped on the massive, gorgeous ring.

"Good, good?" he asked.

That was what I would have to be satisfied with. Not perfect. Not blissful. But good. And, for me, after every mistake I'd made along the way, that should certainly be enough.

I smiled. "Good, good."

"You got a delivery," Eloise announced.

I looked at the package, not sure what it was, as I hadn't been expecting anything. I set the box of rings beside it, fanning out my fingers.

"What do you think?" I asked.

Eloise's eyes widened. "I've never seen anything like it."

"Well, they made twenty-five different rings for this, all one of a kind. A bit over the top, but I'm glad this one was in there. Easily one of my favorites."

"It looks beautiful on you, miss." She smiled at me. "Is there anything else you need or would you rather be alone?"

"Alone for now, I think."

"Excellent. Call when you're ready for dinner, and I'll be right up."

I nodded, and she disappeared around the door, the hem of her dress hitting it as she left.

I never should have doubted Neena.

I gripped the back of the chair at my table, trying to take things one breath at a time. I'd nearly lost so much, but I had to remember how much I'd gained. I was queen, and I was engaged. I'd finally learned what it was to see other people and what it meant to let other people see me. I still had so much to accomplish, so many things I wanted to do for my family and for my people. I hoped I'd firmly settled myself in a place where I could do that.

Sighing, I curiously unwrapped the thin box in front of me. I slid off the lid and gasped.

Staring back at me was a beautiful image of my family on coronation day. Osten looked like he was plotting something mischievous as always, and Ahren was so handsome. All Kaden needed was a sword in his hand, and the image of a perfectly gallant prince would have been complete. I flipped to the next picture, and we were there again in a slightly different pose. I tore through the box, taking in shot after shot, beaming with happiness. Lady Brice clenched me in a hug, Kile laughed as he cradled me in his arms, and the Legers stood with a hand on each of my shoulders as if I really was their daughter.

These moments felt so far away now. It was almost as if I was looking at another girl in all these photos. A little time and hope was all it took to change a person.

When I got to the pictures with Eikko, they stood in stark

contrast to all the others. I'd taken off my cape and he was in his vest, and I realized that I had subconsciously posed us like two people in love. My hand rested on his chest as he held onto my waist, and my head was tilted slightly toward him, like his heart had a gravitational pull.

I stared at my favorite picture for a very long time, thinking how amazing it was that the photographer had captured the light in his eyes. Just hours after this was taken, I'd stared into those eyes, been held by those arms. How remarkable was it that I had this picture at all? Had it not been for the others, he might not have even walked over with me, whispering Finnish in my ear. I told myself that I'd been lucky we met in the first place. Had I fought my parents, had Henri not been brave enough to apply, had I moved my hand two inches to the right when I pulled out his envelope . . .

I took the photo and walked over to the drawer where I'd been hiding my treasures. I smiled, looking down at my little collection and remembering the past two months with a sense of gratitude.

Henri's shirt that he made into an apron. Kile's hideous tie that prevented world peace. Hale's pin, stabbed through a scrap a fabric, reminding me to keep it together. Fox's embarrassing stick-figure drawing. Gunner's poem that I really didn't even need on paper because I couldn't forget it if I tried. These were the things I'd saved.

I stood there, the photo hovering above the drawer. As much of a treasure as this picture was, I couldn't drop it in. There was no way I could put my Eikko in a box.

CHAPTER 32

BEFORE WHAT WOULD BE THE most important day of my life could even begin, I was summoned to the Women's Room. My mother could have held court anywhere, and I still didn't understand what made some massive parlor her favorite place to do it. All the same, she had called, and I was coming.

Miss Lucy was there, and so was Aunt May. I didn't know who let slip the news to her, but I was so thrilled I nearly bolted across the room to her. But then I saw that my beloved aunt was not the reason I'd been called. Miss Marlee was weeping into Mom's shoulder.

She looked up and zeroed in on me. "If you didn't want to marry him, fine, but why—WHY—did you banish him? How am I supposed to live without my children?"

"Josie will still be here," I reminded her gently.

She held up a finger at me. "Don't get smart. You may be

queen, but you are still just a child."

Mom's eyes darted between us, unsure what to do: defend a daughter who was old enough to defend herself but her daughter nonetheless, or comfort a friend whose son was leaving her with very little warning—a pain she understood intimately.

"Miss Marlee, you have to let me explain." I crossed the room, watching her crumple into a chair. "I love Kile. He's become more precious to me than I ever could have expected. And the truth is, he would have stayed for me. He might have even stayed for you. But did you really want that?"

"Yes!" she insisted, looking up at me with red eyes.

"It almost literally broke my mother's heart when Ahren left. It broke mine. Does that mean he should have stayed here forever?"

She didn't answer that. I saw that Mom's eyes were downcast, and she pursed her lips, like maybe she was only understanding this herself now.

"I know we're not supposed to talk about the things that make us uncomfortable. Like how your hands ended up covered in scars," I said, staring Miss Marlee down. "But we need to talk about it. It's remarkable what you did for love, and I am jealous of and awed by you."

Her face pulled together, tears spilling again, and I fought to keep myself together. I had too many people counting on me today.

"We all know what you did, and we all know how you

were restored, and I understand that you think you are somehow permanently indebted to our family, but you're not. Miss Marlee, what else do you think we could want from you?"

She still said nothing.

"Ask my mother. She doesn't want you trapped here. You can go with your son if you want to. You could travel the world as dignitaries if you like. To think that because your life was spared it is no longer yours is a lie. And to pass that burden on to your children? To make a gifted, talented, passionate young man spend his best years cooped up behind these walls? That's cruel."

Miss Marlee's head fell into her hands.

"You could have gone," Mom whispered to her. "I thought you knew."

"It didn't feel like that, not for me. Carter and I would have died years ago if it wasn't for you and Maxon. I didn't feel like I could ever not be in the process of thanking you."

"You befriended me when I was a stranger. You talked me down from walking out of the Selection. You held back my hair when I had morning sickness. Remember, because it always happened in the afternoon?"

They both laughed.

"When I was scared of this job, you told me I could do it. You helped stitch up a bullet wound, for crying out loud."

I was about to ask about that one but chose to let it go.

Miss Lucy walked over and knelt beside Miss Marlee, taking her hand. "We have a very tangled past, don't we?" she said. Mom and Miss Marlee smiled. "We've made mistakes and kept secrets and done plenty of foolish things along with the good. But look at us. We're grown women. And look at Eadlyn."

The three of them did just that.

"Should she be looking at herself twenty years from now bound by every little lapse in judgment? Feeling chained by them?"

I swallowed.

"Should we?" Miss Lucy concluded.

Miss Marlee's shoulders slumped, and she pulled Mom and Miss Lucy close.

I watched this, feeling a knot in my throat.

A day would come when my mother would no longer be here, when my aunt could no longer visit, and these ladies would move away. But then there would be me and Josie and Neena, with daughters and cousins and friends. We would live together and weave our lives into one another's and hold on to a sacred sisterhood that only a handful of women ever experienced.

And I was glad that my mom had chosen to come here, across the country, to the home of a stranger, and trusted a girl on a plane and befriended the girl who drew her baths, and that no matter if and when they parted, they would never be separated. Not really.

CHAPTER 33

THE STUDIO HAD BEEN GIVEN a makeover. While discussing my engagement in front of an audience of friends, family, and staff members as I was broadcast live across the country wasn't exactly the level of intimacy I'd been aiming for, sometimes a girl just has to take what she can get.

I searched the room, looking for Mom and Dad. I needed to see them, to see their smiles at my choice. If they were happy and calm, then I could be, too. But they weren't here, yet. Kaden, however, was.

I watched from the door, seeing him stare across the room as if he'd been slightly bewitched. He spooked a little when I came up next to him.

"You okay?"

He cleared his throat and looked down at his feet, blushing.

"Yeah, everything's great. Just hanging out."

I followed his gaze to see if I could figure out what he'd been looking at, and it instantly became all too clear. Josie had given up on elaborate hairstyles and excessive jewelry. She'd abandoned heavy makeup and showy gowns. Looking at her now—hair slightly curled, the hint of gloss on her lips, and an age-appropriate blue dress—it seemed she was finally stepping into her shoes instead of mine.

"Josie's really pretty tonight," I commented.

"Oh? I hadn't noticed. But now that you mention it, yeah, she looks nice."

Miss Marlee, seeming breezy and peaceful, said something to Mr. Carter, and Josie laughed, the sound still a little too loud for my ears but pretty nonetheless.

"Since you're not on camera for the show, maybe you should go sit with her. It looks like she's got an open seat." I peeked down at Kaden, watching a little smile twitch onto his face before he covered it back up again.

"I suppose. I mean, I don't really have plans to sit with anyone else."

He walked over to her, straightening his suit the whole way, and I found myself dying to know how all that would unfold.

"Eadlyn."

I turned to Mom's voice, happy to see her coming over with open arms.

"How are you feeling?"

"Totally wonderful and not at all terrified," I joked.

"Don't worry. Henri's a good choice. An unlikely one, but very good still."

I peeked to the back of the room where Eikko was straightening Henri's tie, and they spoke back and forth, their lips a jumble of shapes I couldn't read.

"What's funny, though, is there's nothing to be jealous about."

I looked up at Mom, confused. "Jealous?"

"Earlier today when you were speaking to Marlee, you said you were jealous of what she did for love."

"Did I say that?" I swallowed.

"You did. And I wonder why you'd be jealous of someone suffering to get to the person she loves when it seems like a very sweet boy is waltzing right into your arms."

I froze. How could I spin this around?

"Maybe a better word would have been *admire*. It's a very brave thing she did."

Mom rolled her eyes. "If you want to lie to me, that's fine, but I'd suggest you stop doing it to yourself before you find you're in a position you can't get out of."

With that she walked on, taking a seat next to Miss Lucy and General Leger. The studio was usually cold, but I felt sure that the chill that went through me wasn't related to the temperature.

"And you'll wait right here," the producer said, dragging Henri to stand beside me. "We still have some time, but don't go running off. Has anyone seen Gavril?" she shouted to no one in particular.

Henri pointed to the tie that Eikko had just fixed. "Is good?"

"Yes." I brushed at his shoulders and sleeves. I looked past him to Eikko, who had done an amazing job at pulling himself together. I hoped I appeared as calm on the outside as he did. Inside it felt like I was a sweater with a loose string being pulled and pulled until I'd be nothing but a knot on the floor.

I walked around Henri under the guise of double-checking his suit from all angles. I dropped my arm as I passed Eikko, and our fingers met in a kiss before I moved back to stand in front of my fiancé.

The thrill running up my skin was electrifying, so I clasped my hands together in front of me, focusing on the feeling of my engagement ring against the back of my fingers. In my periphery, Eikko's figure disappeared through the crowd, presumably so he could find his own level of sanity in this moment.

"So," I asked, facing Henri, "are you ready?"

He looked at me, his usually jubilant expression dim. "Are you?"

I wanted to say yes, and I could hear the word in my head, but I couldn't manage to work it down to my mouth. So I just smiled and nodded.

He saw right through me.

Taking my hand, he pulled me toward the back of the room, toward Eikko.

"*En voi*," Henri said, his tone more solemn than I'd ever heard it.

Eikko's eyes flashed between us. "*Miksi ei?*"

"I am slow here," Henri said, pointing to his mouth. "Not here." He pointed to his eyes.

My breathing sped up, knowing my life was all about to fall apart, and terrified of what might happen after it did.

"You are love," he said, motioning between us.

When Eikko started to shake his head, Henri sighed and picked up his right hand, pointing to the signet ring. And then he picked up mine, which still wore Eikko's.

"Eikko, please explain to him. I have to follow through with my Selection. Tell him he'll never need to doubt me."

Eikko rattled off my appeal quickly, but Henri's expression remained undeterred.

"Please," I pleaded, grabbing onto his arm.

His expression was incredibly sweet when he spoke. "I say no." He picked up my hand and gently pulled off my engagement ring.

The room started turning fuzzy at the edges. I was minutes away from a live announcement, and I'd just been jilted.

Henri grabbed my face, looking deeply into my eyes. "Love you," he vowed. "Love you." Then he turned and clutched Eikko's arm. "And love you. My good friend. Very good friend."

Eikko swallowed, looking ready to cry from Henri's words. Through most of the last two months, all they'd had were each other. Forget what this moment meant for me.

What did it mean for them?

Henri pulled us both in close. "You being together. I make your cake!"

Despite my worries, I laughed. Looking into Eikko's eyes, I ached to let go and give my heart the one thing it truly wanted. But I couldn't get past my fear.

I scanned the room, searching for the one person I needed right now. When I found him, I turned to my boys. "Wait here. Please."

I ran across the studio. "Daddy! Dad, I need your help."

"Sweetheart, what's wrong?"

I took a deep breath. "I don't want to marry Henri. I want to marry Eikko."

"Who?"

"Erik. His translator. I'm in love with him, and I want to marry him. And even though he hates having his picture taken, I want to take a thousand so I can put him on my wall and wake up to us laughing every day, just like you do with Mom. And I want him to make me doughnuts, just like his mom does for his dad. Even if I have to let out all my dresses. And I want us to find our own thing or maybe find out that our own thing is everything, because I feel like if I have him, even the stupid stuff would matter."

He stood there, mouth slightly agape.

"But a word from you and I'll never mention it again. I want to do the right thing, and I know you'd never let me do something stupid. Tell me what I should do, and I won't question it, Dad."

He looked up at the clock, his eyes still wide with shock. "Eadlyn, you only have seven minutes."

I followed his gaze, and he was right. It was seven 'til.

"So help me. Tell me what to do!"

After a stunned second, he turned back to me and pulled me out the studio door.

"We all know that you wanted to move fast because of Marid, and I think there's some value to your line of thought. But you can't let one bully decide the rest of your life. Trust me. You don't have to announce anything today."

"That's not the point. I want to be with Eikko so much it hurts, but I've done so many selfish, idiotic things in the past that I fear the people won't forgive me if I break even the tiniest rule. I can't bear to let them down, Dad. I can't bear to let you down."

"Me? Let me down over a silly little rule?" He shook his head. "Eadlyn, you come from a long line of traitors. You couldn't let me down."

"What?"

He smiled. "Your brother running off to France was technically enough to start a war over. I think he knew that. Did it stop him?"

I shook my head.

"Your mother," he said with a laugh. "She conspired with the Italian government to fund the Northern rebels, a move that would have sent her to her grave had my father found out."

I stood there, stunned.

"And me? I've been keeping someone who ought to be

dead alive for over twenty years."

"The Woodworks?" I guessed.

"Ha! No, I forgot about them, though officially they were pardoned. It's actually someone much more dangerous in the eyes of the monarchy."

"Dad, I don't understand."

He sighed, looking up and down the hall, checking for spying eyes, before quickly unbuttoning his shirt. "I'm afraid there's only one way to explain this." He turned around and swiftly shoved his shirt down along with his suit coat.

I gasped in horror as I took in my father's back. He was covered in marks, some wide, as if they'd healed without any treatment, and some skinny and puckered. There didn't appear to be any uniformity to the marks except that they all must have come from the same cane or whip.

"Daddy . . . Daddy, what happened to you?"

"My father happened to me." He pulled his shirt back on and buttoned it as fast as he could, speaking in a rush. "Sorry I never took you to the beach, honey. I just couldn't do it."

My posture sank. Of all the things to apologize for. "I don't understand. Why did he do that to you?"

"To keep me in line, to keep me quiet, to make me a better leader . . . he had a myriad of reasons. But there are only two of these beatings you need to know about. The first is one that happened after your mother proposed we eliminate the castes."

He shook his head, almost smiling as he remembered. "She chose to say this on a *Report* while she was still in the Selection. Of course my father, who already hated her, saw

this as a threat to his control. Which it was. Such a suggestion is treasonous. Like I said, it runs in the family. I worried
he would punish her, so I let him take it out on me instead."

"Oh, my goodness."

"Indeed. That was the last beating I ever endured, and for
the life of me, I'll never regret it. I'd take it a hundred times
over for her."

I'd never known about that. All I'd ever known was that
they took on caste elimination together. So many of the
unpleasant details of their history had been glossed over.
There was plenty of awful along with the wonderful.

"I almost hate to ask, but what was the other one I needed
to know about?"

He snapped the last of his buttons and sighed. "The first
one."

I swallowed, unsure if I wanted to hear this story or not.

"You see, my father was a very conceited man. He thought
the world owed him everything because he was king. And,
really, he had no reason to be unhappy. He had power, a
wonderful home, a wife who adored him, and his very own
son to carry on the line. But it was never enough."

His eyes stared unfocused, and I watched him, still not
understanding. "I always knew when his mistress was coming. He'd give my mother a gift earlier in the day, as if he
was paying for his sins before he committed them. Then, at
dinner, he'd fill her wineglass over and over until she was
ready to pass out. And, of course, she kept her quarters in
the other wing. I assume that was his idea, not hers. I can't

imagine her ever intentionally separating herself from my father. Genuinely, she worshipped him.

"Anyway, I was eleven or so when I was walking through the palace and caught her leaving one night, hair a mess and a cape over her shoulders as if she could cover up what she'd done. I knew. I knew why she was there, and I hated her for it. More than I hated him, which was unfair. As soon as she was gone, I went to my father. He was in his robe, drunk and sweaty. And I said to him—I'll never forget it—I said, 'You cannot let that whore in here again.' As if I could tell the king what to do.

"He grabbed me by my arm so hard he dislocated my shoulder. He put me on the floor and caned me across the back I don't know how many times. I was so dizzy with pain, I passed out. I woke up in my room with my arm in a sling. As I came to, my butler said I shouldn't roughhouse with the guards, that I was too young to consider them playmates."

Dad shook his head. "I don't know who got fired or worse to make that story seem legit, but I knew I was supposed to keep quiet. And I was so small, I didn't dare risk telling anyone. As I got older, I hid it because of shame. And then, somehow in my head, I turned it into something to be proud of. I endured this suffering alone, without support, and that was something admirable. Of course, it wasn't. It was stupid, but we make excuses for ourselves when we're small."

He gave me a weak smile.

"I'm so sorry, Dad."

"It's okay. It's made me a stronger person and, I hope, a

better parent. I hope I've done right by you."

My eyes welled. "You have."

"Good. Well, to answer your question, a few years later I thought my father really had gotten rid of his mistress. As I said, I knew when he was planning to bring her, and I watched for him to go into the old routine and even snuck out several nights just to be sure. She was gone for months and months, and then, one day, there she was, walking down the hallway as if she owned the place.

"I was filled with so much anger at this woman, irate that she had the gall to show her face while my mother slept just around the corner. So I stopped her and told her something to that effect. She cocked her head and smirked at me, like I was a bug, like I was nothing. Then she lowered her face to my ear and whispered, 'I'll tell your little sister you said hello.' And she walked away, leaving me completely gob smacked. I must have stood there for a solid ten minutes, too stunned to move.

"Did she say that simply to make a dig at me? Did I really have a half sister I didn't know about? I wasn't going to beg her for answers, and it was clear that I couldn't go to my father. It wasn't until after he died that I could even attempt to look for her."

He swallowed. "Here's the thing, though. Illegitimate children of a royal family member are not allowed to live."

"What? Why?"

"I think because they might cause a threat to the royal line. Civil war or political unrest does no one any good.

Even now, look at the trouble Marid has made. So in the past we eliminated those threats as soon as they were discovered." He said all this coldly, disconnected in a way.

"So did you kill her?"

He smiled to himself. "No. I was enchanted with her the moment I laid eyes her. She was just a child, and she had no idea who her father was. It wasn't her fault she'd been born half royal. So I took her away from her mother, kept her near me, and have been protecting her ever since."

He finally risked meeting my eyes.

"Lady Brice?" I asked.

"Lady Brice."

I didn't know what to say. I had another aunt. And she'd done as much for me as anyone else in my family recently. More than some, really. I was indebted to her.

"I feel bad keeping her in the shadows," he admitted.

"I know. If she has royal blood, I feel like she deserves more."

"It's not possible. And she understands that. She's thankful enough to be here," he answered. And though we both knew the truth of it, I could see we didn't agree that it was satisfactory. "So you see, I have committed treason every single day for the last twenty years. Your mother has, your brother has. I dare say Kaden might be the only one who makes it out without ever breaking a rule."

I smiled at the truth to that, dreading just how many Osten would destroy.

"Break the stupid rule, Eadlyn. Marry the man you love. If

he's good enough for you to approve of, then I certainly do. And if the people don't, that can be their problem. Because who are you?"

"I'm Eadlyn Schreave, and no one in the world is as powerful as me," I blurted without thought.

He nodded. "Damn right you are."

The producer burst through the door. "Thank goodness! You have ten seconds. Run!"

CHAPTER 34

I BOLTED INTO THE ROOM, searching for Eikko. I couldn't see him through the throng of people who'd been scurrying around hunting for me.

I tripped onto the stage as the light on the camera turned red, and I brushed my hair out of my face as I began speaking with absolutely no idea where my words would take me.

"Good evening, Illéa." I broke all the rules I'd learned about public speaking. My posture was atrocious, my tone was uneven, and I didn't bother looking into the camera because I was too busy searching for Eikko. "We have a bit of a surprise for you tonight. On this special edition of the *Report*, I have an important announcement."

Finally I spotted him, half tucked behind Henri.

"Please join me in welcoming Mr. Eikko Koskinen to the stage."

The room applauded, and I stood there hoping he'd brave the cameras for me. Eikko swallowed and straightened his tie as Henri patted his back, urging him to move.

I took his hand and invited him to stand beside me, feeling a little light-headed and worried that he may be feeling the same way.

"Some of you might remember this gentleman from a *Report* a few weeks ago. He is Sir Henri's translator, and since his arrival at the palace, he has proven himself intelligent, kind, honorable, funny, and a dozen other things I didn't realize I wanted until I saw them in him." I looked over, and something about his expression, the hopefulness in his eyes, calmed me. I forgot about the cameras. "As such, I've fallen hopelessly in love with him."

"And I with you," he answered so quietly, no one may have even noticed.

"Eikko Petteri Koskinen, would you do me the extraordinary honor of becoming my husband?"

He let out one beautiful, disbelieving laugh, and the world stood still. There was no falling to knees or scrambling for rings. It was just him and me.

And millions of people watching.

He turned, and I followed his eyes, knowing he was looking for Henri. His friend stood there waving his hands and mouthing *yes* exaggeratedly, wild-eyed.

"Yes," Eikko finally said, laughing as he answered.

I flew at him, wrapping my arms around his neck and pulling him in for a kiss. I was vaguely aware of applause and whistles, but the joyful pounding of my heart drowned out most of it.

A corner of my mind told me I should be worried about how the country might react, how things would unfold after tonight. But the rest of me silenced that worry, and I knew, with pure and perfect certainty, that I'd found my soul mate.

I pulled back to look at him, indescribably happy.

After a second, confusion settled on his face. "So . . . what do I do now?"

I smiled. "Just stand to the side for a moment. I have something else to take care of. And then so much I want to talk to you about."

"Same here."

The clapping dimmed, and I stared into the camera, too content to be afraid anymore, and told my people the truest thing I knew.

"I am aware that I've only been your queen for a few days, but in that short while, and for a long time before, I have been very worried about my place in your hearts. I'm not sure I'll ever understand why I've come up against such disapproval, but I'm only now seeing that I shouldn't care. My life should be wholly mine, not yours.

"And, conversely, your lives should be wholly yours, not mine."

In that moment I felt the mood in the room shift, and maybe I was crazy, but it felt like it was bigger than what I could see in the studio.

"These last two months have been a whirlwind for me.

I've made it through nearly losing my mother, having my beloved twin move abroad, being crowned queen, and finishing a Selection none of us expected me to have." I smiled, thinking of how fast it all happened, how it should have torn me apart but didn't.

"Through all this, some of you have been sympathetic, while others have felt ignored. Some have been supportive, and others have been aggressive. Until recently I would have said those feelings had no foundation, but I am sure now that is untrue.

"Before the Selection I lived my life within a small circle of acquaintances. I admit, my greatest concern in the world was my own comfort, and to maintain it I was willing to sacrifice a vast pool of things, including the well-being of so many around me. I'm not proud to tell you this."

I focused on the carpet for a moment, needing to steady myself. "But meeting these young men showed me a world beyond the walls that I enclosed myself within. It is only in these past few weeks that I have learned how little I knew about my own country. Budgets and proposals can give me a blueprint of your needs, but it has been seeing you face-to-face that has shown me how much more you are up against.

"As such"—I took a deep breath—"I come before you now to announce that Illéa will become a constitutional monarchy."

There were gasps and murmurs around the room, and I gave them a moment to settle, imagining those watching at home needed the same consideration.

"Please don't see this as me shirking my duties. In truth, I know now that I love you too much to attempt to do this job alone. Even with a partner," I said, peeking over to Eikko and smiling, "it would be far too great for anyone, as has been shown by the young deaths and health issues of my predecessors. I will do my part so that you can do yours.

"For so long now we here in the palace have searched for ways to make your lives better, happier, only to find that there is no way for us to do that. Your lives need to be in your hands. Only then will we see the change so many of you have waited through generations to see.

"I will find a suitable prime minister in the interim, and we will plan to hold proper elections within the next two years. I cannot begin to express how eager I am to see what you have in store for our country."

"I'm sure there will be many questions and hiccups as we reinvent our country, but please know that we in the royal family are on your side. I cannot govern your hearts any more than you can govern mine. I think it is time for all of us to seek out a brighter and better future."

I smiled, not feeling fear or anxiety, but a sense of peace. If any of us had stopped worrying about how we *looked* like we were performing and focused on how we were actually performing, we would have come to this conclusion long ago.

"Thank you so much for your support. For me, for my family, and for my fiancé. I love you, Illéa. Good evening."

I watched as the lights on the cameras went out, and I stepped off the set to a flurry of shouts. The advisers were angry, obviously, turning to my father and demanding answers.

"Why are you yelling at me, you fools?" he called back at them. "She's your queen, for goodness' sake. Ask her."

I turned to Eikko.

"Are you all right?"

He laughed. "I have never been happier or more terrified."

"That sums it up pretty well."

"Hey!" Kile called, with Henri coming up behind him to embrace Eikko. As they began celebrating, I moved away. There was much more that needed to be taken care of.

I elbowed my way past confused and irate advisers, dialing a familiar number on the phone in the back of the studio.

Marid picked up instantly. "What did you just do?" he screamed.

"I uninvited you from any participation in my reign."

"Do you realize how stupid that was?"

"What I realized was that something perfectly normal completely horrified you a few weeks ago. It makes sense now. Why would you want power in anyone's hands but yours?"

"If you think this will be the last you've heard from me—"

"Indeed I do. For my ear is now closer to my people, so I have no need of you. Good-bye, sir."

I smiled, positively blissful, now knowing this very important thing: my country could never be taken from me now; I'd happily given it away. My people wanted happiness as much as I did, and I was sure we were all done with people trying to live our lives for us.

"Eadlyn!" Lady Brice called, rushing in to me. "You brilliant, brilliant girl!"

"You'll do it, right?"

"Do what?"

"Be prime minister. It's just until we have elections, but still."

She chuckled. "I'm not sure I'm the best person for the job. Besides, there are—"

"Come on, Aunt Brice."

For a split second she looked absolutely horrified. Then her eyes swam with tears. "I never thought I'd get to hear those words."

I reached for her, embracing this woman who'd become one of my greatest confidantes. It was strange because, even though I'd never lost her, holding her now felt a lot like getting something back. Like when Ahren came for the coronation.

"Oh, my goodness, I have to call Ahren!" I exclaimed.

"We'll add that to the list of things to do. Get engaged, check. Change the country, check. What's next on the agenda?"

I looked across the room, watching my father shake Eikko's hand and Mom reach up to kiss his cheek.

"Changing my life."

EPILOGUE

IT'S A FUNNY THING TO be the product of a fairy-tale romance. It's another thing to think you might find one yourself. You can read the stories and watch the movies, and you can think you know how it's all supposed to unfold.

But the truth is, love is as much fate as it is planning, as much a beauty as it is a disaster.

Finding a prince might mean kissing a lot of frogs. Or kicking a lot of frogs out of your house. Falling might mean running headfirst into something you always wanted. Or dipping your toe into something you've been scared of your whole life. Happily ever after could be waiting in a field a mile wide. Or a window as narrow as seven minutes.

ACKNOWLEDGMENTS

OKAY, Y'ALL. I FEEL LIKE by this point I could give you a pop quiz on the people who end up on my acknowledgments page and you would ace it. You follow my agent on Twitter and tag my publicist on Tumblr and think my editor is my sister even though she isn't. You also ask about my hubby and kiddos when I do signings, because they've started mattering to you, too. So let's just keep this simple.

Thanks.

To the army of people who make the books beautiful, to the friends and family who keep me going, and to you. This series has been the ride of a lifetime, and if we never have anything as much fun as this, I'll still be happy.

And thanks to America and Eadlyn for deciding to live in my head. Changed my world.

I love you forever.

—K

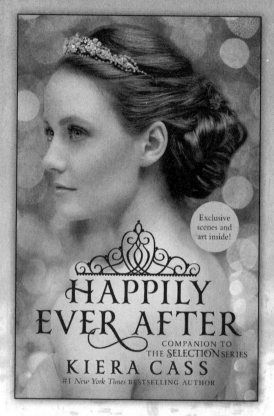